FOREWORD

Gerry Anderson was a pro
of science fiction and
Supermarionation shows from Thunderbirds to Joe 90 via
Captain Scarlet, were all produced in the 1960s bringing him
huge success in the UK. In the 1970s he looked further afield.
His two live action shows, UFO and Space: 1999 were produced
with more than one eye on the American market. Space: 1999
in particular saw the casting of a bona fide Hollywood star in
Martin Landau. This was cemented with the involvement of
US writer and producer, Fred Freiberger. Freiberger already
had an impressive pedigree from his work on shows like Ben
Casey, The Wild Wild West and Star Trek. Perhaps unfairly,
he is often blamed for the decline in the quality of Star Trek
in its last series, just as he is often blamed for the decline in
the fortunes of Space: 1999 in its second. Whatever the truth,
Gerry Anderson was obviously keen to maintain their working
relationship: Intergalactic Rescue 4 was the result.

Pitched as 'A Television Series for Saturday Morning', IGR4
was a blend of Anderson's familiar theme of heroic rescue and
the more saccharin American approach where every story
should have a sugar-coated moral. Running over 10 episodes,
it was to follow the adventures of two teenagers, Jason Stone
and Anne Warran, and two robots on board their eponymous
spaceship. It's unclear whether it would have seen a return to
the marionettes of Anderson's heyday, been his first animated
production or a continuation of his live action shows. Gerry's

son, Jamie Anderson, suggests it may have been the latter, which would have made for a very interesting prospect.

It was Jamie who first sent me the treatment of Intergalactic Rescue 4. It's quite a long document covering the premise of the series, the characters and – in particular – the ship itself; everything from the armaments it carries (it is stressed they are to be used 'strictly for rescue work') to where the two teenagers sleep. Outlines then follow of each of the 10 stories in wildly varying degrees of detail. From the word count alone, it is clear which stories excited them most. Some are merely sketched out with phrases such as 'they rescue them' or 'they escape', while others go into baffling detail about Einstein's Special Theory of Relativity. There is no dialogue, very few of the characters are named other than the main protagonists and, just sometimes, the 'in-universe' continuity is a little contradictory. I've tried to clean up the inconsistencies (while no doubt inadvertently introducing some new ones of my own) and put a little more flesh onto the bones of those unnamed characters. I've also tied the whole thing up with a 'series arc' which I hope will add a little mystery and convince you to read on to the very last adventure.

You can find out more about the changes I have made and why in my 'Author's Note' at the back of this book. However, I urge you not to flick ahead and read them first because, by their very nature, they contain spoilers!

Like my previous novelisation of Gerry Anderson's Five Star Five, it is a privilege to be entrusted with bringing another lost project to life. But unlike Five Star Five, Intergalactic Rescue 4 was not a completed screenplay leaving me much more room to add ideas and themes of my own. I hope you judge it a success.

Richard James

STELLAR PATROL

GERRY ANDERSON'S
INTERGALACTIC RESCUE 4

STELLAR PATROL

By Richard James

Edited by Stephanie Briggs

ANDERSON
ENTERTAINMENT

Anderson Entertainment Limited
The Corner House, 2 High Street, Aylesford, Kent, ME20 7BG

Intergalactic Rescue 4: Stellar Patrol by Richard James.

Hardback edition published in 2022.
Paperback edition published in 2022.

www.gerryanderson.com

ISBN: 978-1-914522-38-3

Editorial director: Jamie Anderson
Editor: Stephanie Briggs
Cover design: Marcus Stamps

Typeset by Rajender Singh Bisht

TABLE OF CONTENTS

THE SLAVE TRADER

The alarm interrupted the small crew of Intergalactic Rescue 4 at their breakfast. Just as Jason and Anne settled down to protein flakes and coffee, it sounded loud and clear against the background hum of the ship's idling Pulse Drive.

'There is a distress call, Master Stone,' explained Alpha.

'You don't say.' Jason winked as he swung his legs from beneath the table.

Anne munched on the last of her cereal as she rose from her seat. 'He means...' she began kindly, 'let's see it on the flight deck please, Alpha.'

The small box-like robot blinked and whirred in response as he relayed the information to the main screen.

Although Intergalactic Rescue 4 was an enormous ship, the flight deck was just a short sprint away from the crew's quarters. Most of the craft's bulk was given over to its vast engines, armaments and equipment stores. Being a multi-purpose rescue vehicle meant there was little room given over to the luxuries of life.

'Gimme the details, Zeet,' Jason barked as he ran onto the compact flight deck. Grabbing at a bulkhead, he swung himself into one of the two pilots' seats with practiced ease.

Zeta pointed at the screen with an extendable arm. The diminutive robot was almost identical in every way to the small droid Jason had just left in the canteen, except where Alpha had been the first model off the production line, Zeta had been the last. Quicker, stronger and more efficient in every way, Zeta fancied himself as the superior specimen. Alpha, much older and therefore much wiser, knew different. He was proud of his advanced years, even choosing to walk with a limp to differentiate himself from his younger counterpart.

'What's up, Zeta?' Anne lowered herself into the second pilot's chair and focussed on the screen before her.

'A stricken vessel of unknown origin is transmitting a distress signal on all frequencies.' A pulsating dot of light appeared on the screen as reams of text scrolled beneath it, detailing its speed and trajectory. Behind it loomed a large planet, a giant swathed with swirling clouds.

'Origin?' asked Jason.

'Unknown.'

'Configuration?'

'Unknown.'

Jason frowned.

'That's quite an erratic course,' Anne whistled. 'Engine blowout?'

'They certainly appear to have lost propulsion,' Zeta agreed.

Jason took a breath, suddenly decisive. 'Then let's get to it. Zeet? Lay in the coordinates.'

'Just a minute,' Anne interrupted. 'Look at that.' She pointed at a text box beneath the flashing dot. 'Their altitude is falling fast. Just how big is that planet, Zeta?'

The box robot whirred and clicked as it calculated a response. 'It has a radius of 85,000 kilometres...'

Jason puffed out his cheeks. 'Jupiter size!' he exclaimed. 'That ship is being pulled right into it!'

Anne nodded, patiently. 'And so would we have been if we'd gone charging in.'

Jason flashed her his most winning smile. 'Point taken,' he said. 'Zeet, recalculate and punch in our best approach route.'

'Carefully,' interjected Anne, a note of caution in her voice. 'I've already had to skip breakfast. I don't want the day getting any worse!'

The stricken craft tumbled helplessly as it fell, held in the grip of the huge planet's gravitational pull.

'I can't get alongside it!' Anne yelled desperately from her controls. 'Its course is too erratic.'

'So pull out!' Jason called from his chair.

IGR4 had traversed the distance to the distressed ship in an instant, its Pulse Drive punching a hole in the very fabric of space. Now, as Anne's fingers flew across the flight controls, it moved to a safe distance from the doomed ship.

'Let's suit up,' Jason spun his chair from the flight console.

'Are you crazy?' Anne's eyes were wide. 'Why don't we just tow it out?'

Jason stopped in his tracks and looked at the small robot at his feet. 'Zeet? What are the odds of success if we put a tractor beam on that craft?'

Zeta whirred and clicked again. 'Owing to the enormous gravitational pull of the planet, a tractor beam would be of negligible use. It might hold the ship for a while but any attempt to tow it out would meet with a point zero zero four chance of success.'

Anne interrupted. 'It'll just pull us in right after it. So how long would we have?'

'We could hold the ship stationary for 29 minutes and 33 seconds,' replied Zeta coolly, his servos whirring.

'Ok,' Jason shrugged. 'That'll be long enough.'

Anne swivelled to her co-pilot. 'Really? Are you seriously suggesting just walking right in?'

'Of course not,' replied Jason with a grin. 'I'll knock first.'

'And what'll you do then?'

'All indications are that there's a problem with the engine,' Jason explained gently. 'If I can fix that, they'll be on their way in no time.'

Anne nodded. To give him his due, Jason was eminently qualified to fix anything. She remembered how he had excelled in the spacecraft maintenance module at the Academy.

It was decided that Jason should take Zeta with him and leave Alpha behind with Anne in charge of IGR4. The older robot was put-out at first, until Anne pointed out that calculating the parameters of the tractor beam was by far the more responsible position.

With the ship held firmly in IGR4's tractor beam, Jason extended the docking arm to the craft's airlock. The beam had at least stopped the ship pitching and rolling. It looked almost sedate, thought Jason as he looked through a viewing hatch beside the docking arm, although he knew it was only a temporary state. A wrist chronometer told him he had just 23 minutes left before IGR4 would relinquish its protective hold and the docking arm would be sheared away.

The short distance traversed in a couple of minutes, Zeta extended a mechanical digit to connect with a service node by the airlock doors. A few turns and the door slid aside to allow admittance. Jason felt the unknown ship's artificial gravity grab a hold of him, his boots making contact with the metal grating on the floor with an audible clang.

'So, where's the welcoming committee?' came Anne's voice over Jason's helmet comms. She was monitoring the situation on a screen back on IGR4, the image being fed directly from Zeta's visual circuits.

'Perhaps they've been told never to answer the door to strangers,' sneered Jason as his robot companion got to work on the inner door. The hatch behind him had slid shut and wall-mounted lights blinked on to illuminate the scene. 'It's nothing special,' he reported back as the inner door rolled back into the wall with a soft click. 'Looks purely functional.'

Jason walked stealthily into the corridor beyond, mindful of the ticking chronometer on his wrist.

'Titanium hull,' announced Zeta to no one in particular. 'Evidence of cannibalisation of parts.'

Jason looked around him as he walked. The robot was right. The walls were lined with mismatched panels and exposed machinery. It seemed to have been cobbled together from countless different ships. No wonder Zeta had struggled to identify it.

'Perhaps I'd better get straight to the engine.' Jason was suddenly worried about just what sort of a mess he'd be confronted with. He had felt confident enough in the face of the expected sublight drive, but now he wasn't so sure. What if the engine was as much of a mishmash as the rest of the ship? He glanced at his chronometer. Nineteen minutes remained. Just as he was calling up the ship's schematics on a wall-mounted computer console, he heard the hiss of an interior door. Zeta had been busy at another control node.

As the door slid back into its housing, Jason took a breath. Before him were a dozen humanoids, each chained to the other with heavy iron links. Shabby, shapeless robes hung from their shoulders. They wore downcast expressions on their heavily browed faces and barely seemed to notice their new visitors.

'Anne, are you seeing this?' Jason breathed. 'Looks like we've got ourselves a slave ship.'

'You've got to get them outta there!' came Anne's voice. 'And you've got less than 17 minutes to do it.'

'Sixteen minutes and 13 seconds,' chimed Alpha over the comms.

'He always was a stickler for detail,' said Zeta with a robot sigh.

Having checked the ship's internal atmosphere, Jason flipped the visor on his helmet. The air was breathable. 'Hey!' he called to the assembled slaves. 'We need to get you out of here!' They turned their heads towards him, clearly struggling to focus on his words. 'Of course,' Jason muttered. 'They're drugged.'

'I would close your visor again if I were you,' exclaimed Zeta suddenly, sniffing the air with his olfactory sensors. 'The atmosphere is laced with a synthetic sedative designed to keep them compliant.'

Jason snapped his visor shut at once and switched on the speaker in his chest unit. 'Everyone, follow me and you'll be fine!'

The strange aliens shuffled their feet towards him, Zeta cutting through their chains with a laser as they passed. 'Quickly!' yelled Jason as he turned to lead the motley band back to the airlock.

'Wait!' called Anne in his ear. 'What about the pilot? Our readings indicate the ship was under manual control before its accident, so there must be a pilot.'

Jason groaned as he thought of the minutes ticking away. Before long, the ship would be ripped from IGR4's docking arm to continue its fall towards the huge planet below. And he'd much rather not be on it when it did.

'Okay!' he called, holding up a hand to get the attention of the alien slaves. 'Where is the pilot?'

Vacant eyes stared back. 'Where is the pilot?' Jason tried again, this time enunciating more clearly. He pointed to the empty seat by the flight controls and, ridiculously, found himself miming steering a ship. Still, there was no response. 'Zeet!' he barked to the diminutive robot at his feet. 'You find the pilot, I'll lead this lot off the ship.'

Zeta beeped in the affirmative as Jason corralled the aliens away. The robot opened a connection to IGR4 and requested an infrared scan of the slave ship. Alpha sent over a live image of the craft and Zeta used his visual circuits to project it onto a nearby wall. The slave ship's systems pulsed red. Zeta could make out the glowing forms of the aliens as Jason led them through the airlock to safety. The engines, crippled as they were, still let off a ferocious heat, glowing white hot on the image before him. Leaning forward on his stubby feet, Zeta could dimly make out something else. There, in the engine room, was another heat signature. From the scale of the image, the robot could deduce its exact size and location. A humanoid, approximately six feet tall was, quite inexplicably, lying on the deck by the fuel input. Seeing that Jason had made it back through the docking arm to IGR4 with his strange entourage, Zeta checked his internal chronometer to see just how much time he had left. Twelve minutes remained. With a whistle, the little robot turned about and deployed his wheels. Lifting his feet from the floor, Zeta trundled from the room at considerable speed, eager to reach the pilot before time ran out.

'I've put the feed from Zeta on the screen,' said Anne as Jason led the alien slaves into the canteen. Freeing himself from his space suit he hung it in its compartment, then joined the aliens by the food dispenser.

'Food,' he explained, slowly. 'Eat if you are hungry.'

One of the taller aliens stepped forward, his hands raised in front of him. Jason saw a strange symbol had been branded on his neck. He noticed that the other slaves watched this man's every move. The alien seemed to look deep into Jason's eyes as if trying to read his thoughts then, quite suddenly, clapped his hands together. At this signal, his fellow slaves fell upon the food in the dispensers, eager for nourishment.

'Thank you,' said the alien, unexpectedly.

Jason blinked in surprise.

'I am Okron. We are from the planet Theka Seven. I speak for my people.'

'We have just nine minutes before we have to let your ship go,' said Anne quickly as she moved between them. 'But we think there is one person left on board.'

Jason nodded. 'Where is your pilot?'

Okron turned to face a screen on the wall as his fellow slaves sat to eat. It displayed Zeta's view from the slave ship. Cluttered corridors whizzed past as the little robot approached the door to the engine room. It opened with a hiss as Zeta pressed a console on the wall to reveal a room full of smoke. Loose cables sparked from the floor. Zeta pressed forward through the heat to find a man lying prone on the floor, his leg trapped beneath a mesh of twisted metal pipes.

'There,' said Okron pointing at the screen. 'And may his death be slow and painful.'

His fellow captives murmured in agreement. Anne noticed several of them make a strange sign across their chest.

'Zeta,' she called into the comms, 'you've got to get him out of there. And quick!'

'His leg is trapped beneath the pipes,' came Zeta's response. The image zoomed in on the twisted cables.

The pilot's moans filled the canteen. 'Please,' he was mumbling, delirious. 'You've got to save me.'

'One of those pipes is the fuel line,' Jason panted, his eyes wide. 'Cut through that and we'll all go nova.'

Anne saw Zeta light up his laser attachment in anticipation of making a cut. 'But which one?' She punched a button on the comms console to speak with the pilot. 'This is Anne Warran from Intergalactic Rescue 4 of The League of Planets. We will attempt to free you, but we need your help.' She leaned in closer to the mic. 'Which of those pipes is the fuel line?'

The pilot grunted as he lifted his head to look down. 'I can't tell you,' he hissed, his jaw clenched with pain. 'I'm a pilot not a goddamn engineer.' With that, he sunk back into a murmuring delirium.

'Jason?' Anne turned to her co-pilot, beads of sweat pricking at her forehead. 'What's your best guess?'

Jason shook his head. 'I can't tell. The engine's cobbled together from so many different components.'

'I thought you were the expert!' Anne pleaded. 'If Zeta doesn't cut him out of there in the next six minutes, the tractor beam will fail and he'll die as the ship hits the planet.'

'That would be too good for him,' said Okron quietly. 'He does not deserve such a quick death.'

Anne wheeled round. 'Who is that man?' she demanded, pointing to the screen.

Okron took a breath and looked at his entourage for encouragement. They nodded, sadly. Okron turned back to his rescuers with a sigh.

'His name is Antar K'osen. He is a slave trader.' He gestured around him. ' We are his merchandise.'

Jason leaned back against the wall. 'Where is he taking you?'

'To the planet below us.' Okron gestured to a monitor where an image of the giant planet turned against the blackness of space. 'There he will sell us to the highest bidder.'

Jason was thinking things through. 'Did you sabotage his ship in an effort to escape?'

Okron shook his head. 'We would be unable to do such a thing. The atmosphere aboard is laced with a chemical that acts like a sedative upon us. It's only now we are aboard your ship that we can think more clearly.'

'So that's why you're loath to save him,' Anne nodded in understanding.

'If you spare his life, you rob us of ours.' Okron's eyes brimmed with tears as he spoke.

Jason looked to Anne. 'What do we do? We can't just leave him to die.'

Anne held his gaze. 'But if we let him live, we're condemning these people to a life in captivity.'

Alpha gave a beep from the floor. 'May I remind you,' he began after the robot equivalent of clearing his throat, 'that Earth Control is clear in this matter? Intergalactic Rescue 4's function is purely rescue. No interference is allowed with the customs and practices of any alien society.'

Jason crouched down to meet Alpha's mechanical eye. 'Customs and practices?' he repeated. 'This is more than some quaint religious belief.'

'We've always done things by the book, Jason.' Anne touched him on the shoulder.

'Sometimes the book is just plain wrong.' Jason rose, angrily. 'If we rescue Antar and send him on his merry way with his cargo, we're complicit in these people's fate.'

'Be that as it may,' Alpha interjected, 'we have just 3 minutes and 27 seconds before the tractor beam fails.'

'We can't just leave him,' Jason planted a fist into his open palm in frustration. A sudden scream filled the air. On the screen, the pilot was writhing in agony.

'Which pipe do I cut?' Zeta was asking. 'Guidance requested.' His laser torch was poised.

'Three minutes, precisely,' Alpha announced from the floor.

Anne wheeled round to see Okron in quiet consultation with his fellow slaves. As they concluded their conversation, they each made the strange sign over their chests.

'I am trained as a rocket scientist,' Okron announced at last. Jason and Anne were speechless. 'Before the slave times, my race lived in relative peace and prosperity on Theka Seven. I lived a life of learning. Then Antar's race came to subdue us. We were forbidden many things; education, employment, freedom. We were made slaves.'

'How?' Anne asked, breathless.

'His people have developed a chemical that induces compliance. That, together with my race's naturally pacifist tendencies, make us the perfect candidates for repression.'

'If you know that ship's systems, you've got to save him,' Jason yelled, desperately. 'Can you really leave a man – *any* man – to die in this way?'

Okron nodded slowly and stepped forward. 'Let me talk to your robot.'

Anne punched the comms button. 'Zeta,' she began, 'the next voice you hear will be Okron, one of the slaves we rescued. Do exactly as he says.' She nodded to the alien beside her. 'Go ahead.'

'First, you'll need to plug yourself into the engine's systems.' He squinted into the screen. 'There's an access portal on the wall to your right.'

The assembled party watched as Zeta turned and trundled to the portal. Uncoiling an appendage from his squat body, he inserted a jack and turned it until it locked into place. The portal beeped in response.

'I'm in,' said Zeta.

'Good,' Okron nodded. 'Now, you'll need to burn off the excess fuel. Purge the tanks.'

Zeta beeped in response as the portal began flashing a warning red.

'Fuel tank evacuation imminent,' came a disembodied voice.

'That is good,' Okron confirmed.

'Alpha,' barked Jason, 'switch screen to exterior view.' He watched as the display changed to show the stricken vessel, held fast in the tractor beam.

'You have just 93 seconds to effect a rescue,' Alpha stated.

'Thanks,' Jason murmured as he watched the fuel escape from the craft in billowing clouds of vapour.

'Now,' continued Okron, his face a mask of concentration. 'You may cut the cables without fear of cutting the fuel line.'

Zeta withdrew his jack from the access portal and sped back to the figure lying prone on the floor.

'Let's see it, Alpha,' commanded Jason, and the view on the screen switched to Zeta's point of view. Several thick cables snaked over the pilot's wounded leg. Cutting just one of them would make it easier to lift the man to safety, but which one?

'Cut the twisted cable to your left. The one that travels beneath the blue duct.' The image zoomed in on an innocuous length of pipe. 'Yes,' nodded Okron. 'That is the one.'

Zeta raised his laser torch and brought it to bear on the cable. With a shower of sparks, it split cleanly in two.

'I can move!' the pilot rasped. 'I can move my leg!'

With a supreme effort, Antar pulled his wounded limb clear of the remaining cables and lifted himself onto his elbows.

'Zeta!' bellowed Anne into the comms console. 'You've got just 40 seconds to get clear!'

'Make it as far as the docking arm and I'll seal the airlock,' added Jason. 'Quick,' he shouted to Anne, 'let's get to the flight deck. I'll need to operate the controls from there.'

As the screen snapped off, the two young pilots sprinted from the room leaving Okron and his fellow slaves standing in a sullen silence.

Jason threw himself into his seat and set about his controls.

'Twenty seconds remain,' offered Alpha as he limped onto the flight deck. 'Do you think he'll make it?'

Anne gave what she hoped was a reassuring smile. 'Yes,' she soothed. Anne knew Alpha wasn't asking about the pilot. 'I'm sure he will.'

'Punch it up on the screen, Alpha!' barked Jason from his chair and, in an instance, Zeta's view of his journey to the docking arm unrolled before them.

'Twelve seconds,' intoned Alpha, as calmly as he could.

The screen showed Zeta's progress through the slave ship. Every now and then, an arm dangled into view at the top of the picture, an indication that the diminutive robot had hoisted the injured pilot onto his robotic shoulders.

'Quicker!' yelled the pilot in panic, and it was all Anne could do not to join him.

'Five seconds.'

The airlock to the docking arm was visible now, and the picture tilted as Zeta scooted round bare cables and equipment that littered the floor.

'Three seconds.'

Anne and Jason held their breath.

'Two.'

'I have reached the airlock,' came Zeta's calm voice from the comms.

'One.'

Jason stabbed at a button. 'I've closed the airlock!'

At that, the screen fizzed to static. The ship jolted dangerously.

'Zeet!' screamed Jason above the noise of rending metal. 'Did you make it?' Silence. 'I've got to let go the tractor beam!'

The ship lurched again.

'We're falling,' panted Anne as she grabbed at the flight console. The cockpit was tilting at a crazy angle. 'Let go the tractor beam!'

'Zeet!' Jason wiped the sweat from his eyes. 'Did you make it?'

'Planetary collision in T minus 24 seconds,' Alpha exclaimed. Anne was sure she could detect a note of concern in his mechanical voice.

'Zeet,' Jason whispered, sadly, 'we gotta go.' He reached out to punch at a button on his console. 'I'm sorry.'

'Docking arm retracting,' said Alpha as the cockpit suddenly quietened.

'Okay,' breathed Anne with relief. 'I'm taking us back to a safe distance.'

With a hum of its engines, Intergalactic Rescue 4 retreated

to a higher orbit. An unnerving calm descended on the flight deck as its three occupants gazed at the image on the screen. The slave ship, free of the tractor beam, was tumbling through the planet's upper atmosphere, a glowing ball of fire. Debris broke away as it burned.

Alpha's visual sensors pulsed gently as he watched. 'When humans experience the loss of another, what do they feel?'

Anne turned to face the robot, her eyes sad. 'We feel an emptiness,' she explained. 'We call it grief.'

Alpha looked downcast. 'Then I feel grief.'

'Well,' came a voice from the doorway, 'I feel fantastic!'

'Zeet!' Jason had a wide grin on his face. 'You made it!'

Zeta was standing proudly in the door, the rather bemused pilot beside him, his leg caked with blood.

'Of course I made it. I'm only sorry my visual feed was interrupted in the docking arm. Static, I guess.'

'We need to get this man to the infirmary.' Anne took the pilot by the arm to lead him away. He hobbled painfully into the corridor beyond, his eyes wide in bemusement.

As Jason followed, Zeta turned to his robot companion. Alpha was beeping gently to express his pleasure.

'Did ya miss me?' Zeta squawked, with a flash of his visual sensors that could only be described as a cheeky wink.

'Miss you?' Alpha responded with a harrumph. 'I barely noticed you were gone.'

'He did what?' Strangely, Antar seemed almost angry. Following his treatment in the infirmary, he had been led to the canteen for some refreshment. He was a squat figure, Anne noticed, used to a planet with a greater gravitational pull. He had a sour looking face and nervous, shifty eyes. As he was handed a plate of flavoured protein, Antar K'osen found himself face to face with Okron and the other slaves.

'This is Okron,' began Jason.

'He is number four zero one,' Antar interrupted, jabbing towards the slave with his fork. 'It says so on his neck.'

Anne noticed Okron cover his branded mark with his robe, suddenly self-conscious. 'He is a scientist,' she said, sharply. 'The only one of us who understood your ship's engines.' She leaned in, almost threatening. 'He saved your life.'

Antar swallowed a mouthful of food. 'Then he is a fool.'

'Perhaps I am,' interjected Okron, sadly. 'But I am an honourable fool.'

Jason turned to the slave leader, eager to calm the situation. 'We will talk with Antar,' he whispered. 'Follow the lights on the wall to the astrodome. We will let you know the outcome soon.' He pushed at a wall console and a line of lights led the way from the canteen.

'We have but one demand,' Okron replied. 'A dinghy to take us home.' He looked at the slave trader with narrow eyes. 'And away from him.'

Jason nodded. 'I'll see what I can do.' Satisfied, Okron led his party from the canteen, following the flashing lights towards the astrodome.

'Consider what that man did for you,' said Jason when they were alone. He was having trouble containing his feelings.

'It is irrelevant.' Antar looked unimpressed. 'It changes nothing.'

'You wouldn't be here now if it wasn't for Okron,' added Anne. 'Surely he deserves something in return?'

Antar spluttered on his food. 'You mean his *freedom*?'

Anne nodded. 'Freedom for him *and* his companions.'

The slave trader pushed his empty plate away and swung back on his chair. 'He called himself honourable.' Anne noticed he couldn't even bring himself to mention the slave's name. 'I too am an honourable man.'

'What honour is there in trading slaves?' Jason scoffed.

In response, Antar pulled a computer pad from his tunic pocket. Stabbing at the screen, he pulled up a text file to show the young pilots.

'My contract,' he explained, 'for the delivery of 12 slaves.' He indicated a phrase towards the bottom of the screen. 'Payment on delivery.'

'It's obscene.' Jason was clenching his fists.

'It's a living,' Antar replied, simply. Slipping the computer pad back into his pocket, he leaned forwards on his elbows. 'I have three children,' he began, 'not much younger than the two of you. Their mother died in the Zargon Wars so I am left alone to provide them with a future.' He gestured to the door. 'Those slaves will provide me with the income I need to send my children to school. It's the biggest run of my career.' He tapped his pocket. 'And the biggest payment.'

Anne pulled up a chair opposite. 'Surely you owe it to your children to show them a better way? How would they feel, knowing they profited from the misery of others?'

'It is the way,' Antar shrugged. 'It always has been.'

Jason rounded on him. 'My father used to say those are the four worst words in the English language.' He planted his palms on the table and leaned in close. 'Just because a thing has always been done a certain way, doesn't make it the *only* way.'

There was a silence as the slave trader contemplated the young man's words. At last, he pushed his chair back from the canteen table and stood. 'I heard word of a dinghy,' he said. 'I would be grateful if you would put it at my disposal so I can fulfil my contract.' With that, Antar swept from the room, leaving Anne and Jason to gaze at one another, dumbstruck.

'Intergalactic Rescue 4's function is purely rescue,' said Anne, softly. 'No interference is allowed with the customs and practices of any alien society.'

Jason shook his head. 'Then tell me,' he hissed. 'Just who have we rescued?'

The astrodome was graced with a large bubble window that protruded from the ship's hull, providing the viewer with an almost 270 degree view of the universe beyond. Jason took in the vista before him, his arm draped gently across Anne's shoulders. Alpha and Zeta squatted on the floor beside them. The crew of Intergalactic Rescue 4 seemed united in solemnity. Beyond the viewing window, the dinghy raced away from the ship and towards the great planet below. Jason and Anne had been powerless to intervene as Antar rounded up his slaves and herded them towards the docking bay. They had watched, helpless, as he fixed their chains with a laser torch and shackled them to the small vessel's walls. Now they stood, disconsolate, as the slave trader departed with his merchandise.

'There was nothing we could do,' Anne whispered, partly to convince herself. 'We did everything by the book.'

Jason was unimpressed. 'How will the universe ever progress if we don't better ourselves? Seems to me that Antar is bound by shackles every bit as restricting as his cargo.'

'We tried.' Anne patted his hand as she spoke.

'Course correction,' squawked Alpha suddenly from the floor.

'What?' Jason peered closer at the stars beyond the window to get his bearings. 'But we're stationary.'

'Not us.' Alpha waved a mechanical arm towards the window. 'Them!'

The two pilots' expressions changed to one of wonder as they saw the dinghy peel away from the planet.

'He's changed his mind!' Anne gasped.

'A new course has been laid into the dinghy's navigational computer.' Alpha clicked and whirred. 'Destination: Theka Seven.'

'The slaves' home planet!' Jason squeezed Anne's shoulders in celebration.

There was the sound of static as the astrodome's comms screen crackled to life. The small party recognised Antar at the controls of the dinghy. Behind him, the slaves were seated, comfortably, their broken chains discarded on the floor.

'Just because a thing has always been done a certain way, doesn't make it the *only* way.' Antar gave the crew a wry smile.

Jason nodded in gratitude.

'But your payment?' Anne asked. 'And your children?'

The slave trader looked around the cockpit. 'I reckon this dinghy will be good for a few thousand credits on the open market. More than enough to get them all through their education.' He leaned in closer to the screen. 'Perhaps they will learn that there is always another way.'

'Take it with our pleasure,' Jason grinned. He nodded to Okron in the seat behind. 'And I hope you get home safely.'

'Thank you,' the erstwhile slave smiled. 'For everything.'

With a final nod, Antar leaned forward to punch the screen off. For a moment, the little crew of Intergalactic Rescue 4 stood in silence.

'That's the first time I've heard you mention your father,' Anne said at last, turning to Jason with kind eyes.

'Really?' her co-pilot replied, nonchalantly. 'Well, he was quite a guy. Zeet? Alpha? We need to look at the main drive.

The couplings need recalibrating.' With that, he slipped his arm from Anne's shoulder and walked from the room, leaving the young woman to gaze thoughtfully out the window and to the stars beyond.

SPACE TRAIN

Having left the busy space lanes of the Solar System, the lumbering cargo vessel traced a lonely path to the quieter reaches of the galaxy. The collection of containers were strung together behind a more modern pilot's cab resembling the great cargo trains of the 20th century. The last compartment of all housed the engines, their thruster cones blazing through the stars. The cargo compartments themselves were interchangeable so that the train could be of any length required. Its captain, Thurlow Guss, had run short trips to Venus with just three or four containers and longer journeys with a hundred. But this was the longest yet. Three hundred and forty-eight cargo compartments had been slung between the cab and its engines. It was practically a planetary system in itself, Guss had quipped as he signed on for duty. He had met his engineer at the space quay and they had gelled at once. Trip Kernow was of a similar age to Guss. Turned out they had grown up in the same city, too. For the first three days of the journey, they had traded stories of Gracie's Coffee Bar on Steer Street and the terrible muzak that she had piped into the restaurant. By day four they were sharing favourite tunes on the ship's music system. By day 10 they were talking of their families. Guss and Kernow were a good team.

'I'm just gonna check the fuel mix for our final approach,' said Kernow on day 120. 'She seems a little juddery.' By now their destination, the planet Vulcan, was looming through the cabin windshield.

Guss nodded and pulled his hat further over his eyes. They had just shared a regulation company lunch and he was feeling sleepy. 'I'll brew us some fresh coffee in a minute.'

Kernow cast him a look as Guss settled back into his seat. 'Sure ya will,' he chuckled.

Guss was snoring even before Kernow had left the cabin. The engineer scratched the stubble on his chin and started the long walk through each compartment to the engines. It was a journey he could almost make in the dark, so familiar he was with it. At least, he mused, they were almost half way through the job. In just two days' time they'd make delivery, load up with Vulcan goods to take to Earth and start the long trek home.

Finally, Kernow made it to the engine compartment. As ever, he kissed the bulkhead for good luck before lifting a deck plate to the fuel pump.

The engine below was antique but serviceable. It hissed and thumped as it heaved the great bulk of the space train through the stars. Lowering himself into the hatch, Kernow grabbed a pair of goggles from a hook and tapped at the fuel mix gauge. Just as he thought, it wasn't perfect. But it would do. 'It is my considered opinion,' the engineer mumbled to himself, 'that we're good to go. At least as far as Vulcan.'

Kernow frowned as a sudden rumbling interrupted his thoughts. Glancing up, he noticed wisps of smoke from the compartment above. The deck plates began to rattle.

The blast was enough to wake Guss. The jolt ran through the length of the ship, shaking him awake in his chair.

'What the–– ?'

Guss threw himself onto the control panel, punching at the buttons for a status report. Just about every screen was flashing red. The drive was out. The ship was barely functioning. Swinging a monitor towards him, Guss stared at the readout. A huge hole had been torn into the side of the engine compartment. He stabbed at the comms panel.

'Kernow? What the hell just happened?' There was no reply. 'Kernow?' he called again.

Spinning back to the monitor, he zoomed in on the debris cloud surrounding the jagged hole in the ship's hull. It was faint at first but, as Guss toggled the controls to sharpen the image, he could just make out the figure of Kernow, turning slowly in the blackness of space, an expression of surprise forever frozen on his face. Horrified, Guss flipped the cover on a button he hoped he would never have to use. In a matter of moments, a distress signal was being broadcast, galaxy wide and on all frequencies.

Jason could barely disguise his disgust. 'What is *that*?'

Alpha was only too happy to provide him with the details. 'That,' he beeped merrily, 'is a multi-compartment freight liner. It is primarily a Z-386 model but our sensors indicate extreme cannibalisation of parts.' Extending an arm, Alpha plugged himself into Intergalactic Rescue 4's systems. A section of the craft on the screen was suddenly illuminated. 'This section is the oldest. Construction records indicate it is over 70 years old.'

'Sheesh,' breathed Jason. 'No wonder they're in trouble.'

'Actually,' Alpha explained, '*this* is why they're in trouble.'

The image zoomed in to show the gaping wound in the ship's engine compartment.

'They're venting drive fluid,' Anne noted from the co-pilot's chair. True enough, a gaseous, milky substance was leaking into space from the hole in the hull.

'Zeet,' Anne called, 'can you calculate the ship's course?'

Even without the engines, the freighter was still clocking up quite a speed under its own momentum.

'Judging from its previous and current trajectory,' Zeta whirred, 'it looks like it is heading straight for Vulcan.' The image zoomed out to show a dotted line indicating the stricken ship's course. Sure enough, a large planet loomed at the craft's ultimate destination.

'When you say *heading straight for Vulcan*,' began Anne, suddenly worried, 'do you mean…?'

'He does!' Alpha interrupted before Zeta could speak. 'Current course and speed indicate a direct impact in a little over three hours.'

'Won't it burn up in Vulcan's atmosphere?' Jason asked hopefully.

'Negative,' barked Zeta, trying to wrestle back control of the conversation. 'The angle of entry is too steep, and many of those cargo compartments are too large.'

Jason gulped. 'Then we better get over there.' He spun his chair to face Anne. 'Any luck with comms?'

Anne shook her head. 'Looks like they're down. Scans indicate one life sign in the cockpit. He was lucky enough to get his distress signal away.'

'He won't have long,' Alpha reported from his cubby hole. 'It looks like life support is down, too.'

'Okay,' Jason was trying desperately to get his thoughts in order. 'Zeet, we need to work out the best way to get in there. I'm guessing we go right in through the cockpit?'

'I wouldn't recommend it,' Zeta buzzed, haughtily.

'Oh?' Jason raised his eyebrows. 'Why not?'

'The cockpit is the newest component on the ship. It is composed of Tritanium alloy,' the little droid explained, patiently. 'We don't have the time to cut through it, even with IGR4's advanced equipment.'

'Then what do you suggest?' Anne leaned forward over the flight deck. 'Cut through one of the compartments?'

In reply, Alpha illuminated a particular cargo container on the screen. It was only two compartments behind the cockpit. 'This is made of Venusian steel,' he beeped, 'still strong, but pliable. We could cut through it in an hour.'

'Then that's where we go in.' Jason turned to his co-pilot as he pulled off his restraints. 'Anne, pull up the ship's cargo manifest while I suit up. It'd be useful to know just what we're cutting into.'

'Will do,' Anne confirmed. 'And I'll try to get a hold of the Vulcan government. If a 300,000 ton cargo vessel is about to crash into their planet, I think they deserve to know.'

'Our long-range telescopes are tracking the freighter.' The face of the Vulcan president filled the screen. He wore an expression of irritation that Anne thought strange. 'What are you going to do about it?'

Anne took a breath. 'Well, sir,' she began, 'we are planning to cut our way into one of the compartments. Our priority is to save the remaining crew member, then bring the ship to a halt.'

The president's eyes narrowed. 'Then your priorities are wrong. Our tracking stations have determined the likely site of impact.' He leaned toward the screen. 'It is our largest city with a population of 4 million. I respectfully suggest that *they* should be your priority.'

'We can't ignore the life sign we've detected in the cabin,' Anne protested.

'Destroy that vessel and you'll save 4 million lives.'

'Yes,' replied Anne carefully. 'But we'd rather save 4 million and 1.'

The president frowned. It was clear he wasn't going to convince her. 'Then the Vulcan government reserves the right to destroy it ourselves, just as soon as it enters Vulcan space.'

Anne nodded, sadly. 'You have that right,' she agreed.

'Might I ask,' the president continued, 'just which compartment you are using to gain entry?'

Anne blinked at such a strange question. 'Two compartments from the cabin,' she said. She noticed the president looking at another monitor. Was he reading from a copy of the cargo manifest? She had found no sign of it during her searches, almost as if the record had been deleted.

'That is well,' the president nodded, seemingly satisfied. 'Then I will leave you to it. But remember,' he jabbed a finger at Anne from the screen. 'Once in Vulcan space, we will use our own discretion.'

Jason was clinging on to the cockpit exterior. Having donned his space suit, he had made good use of its built-in retro thrusters to manoeuvre his way across the gulf between IGR4 and the space train. As Alpha and Zeta made their way to the chosen compartment, Jason took the opportunity to try and make contact with the ship's pilot.

Guss was weakening. With oxygen levels running low, he had climbed into one of the onboard space suits in order to make use of its own self-contained breathing apparatus. It might just buy him some time. As he settled back in his chair to conserve his energy, he was surprised to see a figure suspended in space beyond the cockpit window. At first he was certain he was hallucinating. Leaning across the flight deck to look further out, he saw a ship keeping pace with his trajectory. He breathed a sigh of relief. With all the computer systems down he hadn't noticed the ship's arrival. It was a rescue attempt. He gave a thumbs up to the young astronaut beyond the glass and tapped his helmet to indicate he had no comms. The young man nodded in response and held his hand out, palms facing down. Relax, he seemed to be saying, help is on the way. With that, Jason clawed his way round from the cockpit, his hands holding tight on whatever they could find.

Jason could see the glow of the robots' arc welders on the outside hull of the ship. Screwing up his eyes, he flicked a switch to activate his visor's light shield. The glare became more manageable and he approached the two droids, busy with their task. Alpha and Zeta were facing each other, two metres apart. Their welding attachments sparked as they made contact with the ship's hull. Circling around each other, they were slowly cutting a circular hole into the metal plating. After a few minutes, Alpha extended another arm. As Zeta finished slicing through the hull, Alpha magnetised his hand and connected to the panel with a *thunk*. At a bleep from Zeta, he pulled the jagged hatch away from the newly created entrance to the cargo compartment and let it float safely away.

'Entry hatch safely completed,' Zeta reported proudly over the comms. 'Would you like to lead the way?'

Jason nodded eagerly and lowered himself gingerly through the hole. Inside, the compartment was dark. Flicking on the torches mounted either side of his helmet, the young pilot looked around to get his bearings. In front of him was a door leading to the main body of the car. A window to one side showed barrels stacked high and deep.

'You seeing this, Anne?'

Back on Intergalactic Rescue 4, Anne peered at the screen. 'Yup,' she confirmed. The screen was connected directly to a feed from Jason's helmet cam.

'What do you think is inside?' Jason asked.

'To be honest,' admitted Anne, 'I'm having a little difficulty getting hold of any type of cargo manifest.'

'Then, we can't even be sure what she's hauling?' Jason was looking through the window to the cargo within.

'Not a clue.' Anne sat back in her chair, suddenly thoughtful. 'Although the Vulcan president seemed to know.'

'Why would he keep something like that to himself, knowing we were going to try and gain access?'

'Beats me,' Anne admitted. 'Just go carefully in there.'

'How long have we got, Zeet?'

Zeta and Alpha joined Jason through the hole. 'If, as you suggest, the pilot is in his space suit, he might have as much as 40 minutes of air, or as little as 20 minutes.'

'If we knew what *model* of space suit,' Alpha added, 'we might be able to be more specific.'

'But then,' interjected Zeta, 'we wouldn't necessarily know how much air was in its tanks to begin with. Regulations stipulate that any reservoir must be at least 80 per cent full while in storage, but —— '

'Okay, I get it,' Jason hissed. 'What you mean is, let's get a move on.'

With that, the two diminutive robots trundled past and took their positions by the interior door to the next compartment.

'The malfunctioning systems have automatically sealed the door,' Alpha reported, his welding torch sparking to life in readiness.

At a nod from Jason, Zeta leaned in towards the door hatch. 'We'll concentrate our fire on the locking mechanism,' he said.

'Just what I was going to suggest,' bleeped Alpha.

As the robots continued with their task, Jason looked to the rear of the compartment. A window in another door looked into the next car and a door beyond that looked into another. There must be hundreds of the things and yet no one knew what was in them. Jason shook his head. It felt to him like someone was hiding something. He had a sudden thought.

'Anne,' he barked into his comms. 'Why don't we go the long way round?'

'How do you mean?' came Anne's voice.

Jason turned to watch the droids complete their work as he spoke. 'Check the insurance certificates for the launch. Follow the paper trail to find out what's on board.'

'Good idea,' Anne agreed. 'I'm on it,'

As the comms clicked off, Jason let out a sigh. 'There's more to this than meets the eye,' he said to no one in particular.

The two robots stood back as the door finally slid open with a clang of retreating security bolts. 'One down,' Zeta said chirpily, 'one to go.'

The little party shuffled forward into the next car.

Once more, Jason was confronted with a window into the cargo compartment. This time, metal boxes were piled high to the ceiling. Jason could see that each one had a combination lock on its side to keep the contents secure from prying eyes.

'And this is the door to the cockpit,' Alpha reported confidently.

Jason nodded. 'Once we're through there, I'll hook up my spare canister and lead him out the way we came.' He tapped the extra cylinder he had strapped to his back.

Zeta beeped. 'Alpha and I will attempt to connect to the ship's systems and slow it down.'

Great, thought Jason to himself. Once the pilot was out,

the two robots would still have almost two hours to correct the ship's course. That was sure to please the Vulcan president.

Onboard Intergalactic Rescue 4, Anne was busy chasing the paper trail leading to the space train's launch some three months earlier. Working backwards from the launch protocols, she had discovered the entire cargo was insured with Mayhew Freight Insurance. She had even unearthed the policy number. Now she was faced with a difficult decision. Mayhew Insurance had hidden the details behind a firewall. With her computer systems training (she had aced the subject at the Academy), it would be a simple matter to hack into the network and dig out the details. But did she have the right? Anne bit her lip as she considered. Just as she had decided she didn't have a good enough reason for such subterfuge, she was drawn back to the screen by a click from the comms system. The president of Vulcan glowered from the monitor.

'Progress report,' he snapped.

Anne checked Jason's cam feed. She could see the two robots cutting through the door to the cabin. 'We're minutes away from rescuing the pilot.'

'Good,' the president nodded. 'Because minutes are all you have.'

'Huh?' Anne was confused.

'Check your scanners, Ms Warran,' the president sneered, 'then get your ship and crew to a safe distance.'

Suddenly concerned, Anne pulled up a live scan of the immediate area. The space train continued on its inexorable trajectory to the planet Vulcan. There was something else. Squinting at the screen, Anne could see two blips arcing from the planet's surface. Missiles. Her eyes grew wide.

'You said we had hours!'

'Our council has decided to err on the side of–– ' He

never completed his sentence. Anne flicked the screen off as he spoke and screamed to Jason.

'Jason! You've got to get out of there, now!'

Jason's voice crackled from the comms panel. 'What's the panic? We're almost through.'

'You don't have time,' Anne panted. 'The Vulcan council has launched missiles at the ship to destroy it.'

'What?' Jason couldn't hide his alarm. 'How long do we have?'

Her fingers dancing over the control panel, Anne pulled up a simulation of the missiles' trajectory. 'Three minutes,' she gasped.

'We've got three minutes to get him out of there!' Jason screamed to the robots.

Zeta had been monitoring the two pilots' communications and was well appraised of the situation.

'Get back to IGR4, Master Stone,' he bleeped. 'Alpha and I can get the pilot out of here.' The two droids completed their task as he spoke. The door to the cabin swung open.

Jason shook his head. 'Never,' he said. He tapped his comms. 'Anne? I want you to give us a countdown to impact.'

'Be quick,' came Anne's voice in response. 'You have two and a half minutes.'

'Okay, Zeet, Alpha,' Jason breathed, a look of determination on his face. 'Let's get in there.'

Guss was barely conscious. 'He's delirious,' said Jason as he checked the readings on the captain's suit. Although he couldn't hear him, he could see the captain mumbling feverishly behind his visor. 'But alive.'

'Er, Master Stone?' Alpha was pointing towards the

cockpit window with a stubby mechanical arm. Jason followed the gesture to see two missiles streaking through space.

'You need to get the captain out of here now!' Zeta was suddenly busying himself by the flight computer.

'What about you and Alpha?' Jason asked, a note of panic in his voice. He hoisted Thurlow Guss to his feet and raised the captain's arm around his shoulder for support. The movement seemed to rouse Guss from his stupor.

Jason gave him what he hoped was a reassuring smile as he led the captain through the cabin door. 'Come with me, quickly.'

As Jason connected his spare oxygen canister, the captain took, long grateful breaths of air. 'My ship,' he flustered.

Even with the captain's failed comms, Jason could read his lips through his visor. 'We'll save it,' he replied with a look to Zeta. The little droid was reaching out with a mechanical arm to hook himself up to the ship's systems. 'Come on!'

As Jason ducked through the door into the first compartment, he heard Anne's voice over his helmet comms. 'Two minutes,' she said, grimly.

'What are you planning, Zeet?' Jason panted as he picked his way into the second compartment, Guss leaning on him for support.

'The ship's primary engines are offline,' Zeta reported back via comms, 'I can, however, get access to the port thrusters.'

'But you can't outrun the missiles!' Jason was at the outside hatch now, cut just minutes before by the two robots. Peering through the jagged hole, he could see IGR4 keeping pace with the space train. A nudge on his suit thrusters and he and Guss should be clear in moments. Glancing to his right, he could see the trails of the two missiles streaking towards their target. He was sure he, Anne and Guss would be safe aboard Intergalactic Rescue 4, but what of Alpha and Zeta?

He bit his lip as he manhandled Guss through the tear in the ship's hull. The captain was more lucid now and able to grab at the hull plates to heave himself through.

'Alpha has enough power to direct to the thruster systems,' Zeta was explaining over comms. 'It should give us enough for a quick but powerful burst.'

'What'll that do to Alpha?' Jason asked, concerned.

'Nothing more than deplete my battery,' Alpha bleeped.

'I hope you're right,' Jason replied. A click on his comms told him Anne had connected.

'One minute, forty seconds.'

Jason tried his best to sound calm as he wound out a short tether from his suit's chest unit. 'We're on our way.' He attached the hook to a loop on Guss's suit. Reaching to the panel on his wrist, Jason punched a button to activate his suit's thrusters and felt a kick in his back as they engaged. Within moments, he was traversing the gulf between the two ships, Guss twisting on the tether beside him. Reaching out a hand to steady the captain, Jason looked back to see the missiles gaining on the space train. 'You'd better be quick, Zeet!'

In the cockpit, Zeta was making his way through the various firewalls to tap into the ship's computers. There was nothing there he hadn't come across before and so, within moments, he had gained access to the port thrusters. 'Systems are operable,' he reported to his droid companion. 'Can you reach the power port?'

Alpha limped towards an alcove at the rear of the cockpit and plugged himself into an access panel. 'I'm in,' he squawked happily.

'Fifty seconds!' came Anne's breathless report over the robot's external speaker.

'How much charge do you have?' Zeta asked his fellow droid.

'I'm at 89.23 per cent,' Alpha responded, efficiently.

'That should be enough.'

'Zeta?' Alpha whirred suddenly. 'Will you be careful?'

Zeta spun round, a softer tone to his mechanical voice. 'I will look after you, Alpha,' he soothed.

Satisfied, Alpha twisted his probe on the control panel. 'Ready,' he bleeped.

'You have 45 seconds to do whatever you're gonna do!' Anne screamed from the speaker.

'Power transfer commencing.' Alpha seemed to lean in towards the console, as if forcing all his energy into the ship's systems. A panel near Zeta suddenly lit up.

'Port thrusters online!' Zeta exclaimed. 'They're at 60 per cent,' he continued, 'but we need more.'

Alpha was shaking where he stood. 'I'm giving you everything I've got.'

'Seventy per cent,' Zeta read from the monitor. '75.'

'Thirty seconds!' Anne yelled from the comms.

'Eighty-five per cent.'

Alpha's visual circuits were dimming. 'Sending... all reserves... to... the thrusters...'

'Ninety-five per cent!' Zeta stood ready to engage the thrusters. Focusing on the cockpit windshield, he could clearly see the missiles just seconds away.

'Ten!' Anne continued her countdown. 'Nine! Eight!'

'Battery... depleted,' Alpha slurred. Out of power, he

slumped towards the console, now nothing more than a heap of metal and circuitry.

'One hundred per cent!' Zeta called in triumph. With that, he engaged the thrusters.

Jason had manhandled Thurlow Guss on board. Once inside the airlock, he reported his situation to Anne on the flight deck, then turned to look out the window back into space. He watched as the space train continued under its own momentum toward the planet Vulcan. The missiles were just moments away. If Zeta's plan failed then both robots would be lost along with the entirety of the ship and its cargo. Jason thought that would suit the Vulcans just fine, but why?

'I can't look.' Guss was climbing out of his suit. He looked almost completely recovered from his ordeal, although his expression was downcast and his eyes full of sadness.

'The one thing I've learned about our droids over there,' Jason said, almost as much to convince himself, 'is that when they say a thing is possible, it generally is.' He craned his neck to try and focus on the space train's cabin but could see no sign of movement. He could only hope the robots had succeeded in their plan.

'Five!' Anne was counting down, her voice echoing around IGR4's comms. 'Four!' Jason could see the missiles almost upon the train. 'Three!'

Suddenly, the space train gave a lurch. Jason saw a blast from its port thrusters, just powerful and long enough to change its course. The correction seemed to ripple through all the compartments, traveling along its length like a wave.

'They've done it!' Jason cried, and even Guss allowed himself a glance through the window. He gasped as he saw the two missiles scream past the space train, only to explode harmlessly some distance away.

'They saved my ship,' Guss exclaimed, gratefully.

Jason nodded, smiling. 'More importantly,' he said, thoughtfully, 'they saved the cargo.' He stepped out of his suit and gestured that Guss should accompany him from the airlock. 'Now, let's go see why the Vulcans were so keen to see it destroyed.'

'Our droids have managed to slow the ship sufficiently to put it in orbit. It's no longer a threat to your people.' Anne was talking with the Vulcan president as Jason entered the flight deck with his guest. The president frowned from the screen.

'You deliberately thwarted our plans.'

'With respect,' Jason began as he swung himself onto his pilot's seat, 'your plan made no sense.' The president raised his eyebrows, clearly unused to being spoken to in such a manner. 'You could easily have detonated those missiles in such a way as to divert the space train's course. Instead, you chose to destroy it.'

'It posed an imminent threat,' the president responded.

'A threat, yes,' Anne agreed, 'but not imminent. We had hours to get control of that ship. As you saw, our robots were more than capable.'

'Yet you chose to try and destroy it rather than give us the time.' Jason's eyes narrowed with suspicion. 'Why?'

The president chose not to answer the point. 'The Vulcan council does not have to answer to you.'

'That's true,' Anne agreed. 'But you do have to answer to The League of Planets.'

The president leaned in, his posture even more threatening. 'In what matter?'

Anne sat back in her seat. Behind his bluster, the president was clearly rattled. 'In the matter of the illegal transportation of Cyclo-9.'

Jason spun round to stare at her, open-mouthed. 'Cyclo-9?'

'But we weren't carrying Cyclo-9,' pleaded Guss, evidently just as surprised by Anne's assertion. 'We wouldn't go near that stuff.'

'It's okay, Captain,' Anne smiled. 'I know you had nothing to do with it.' She looked suddenly serious. 'But your crewmate's death was a direct result of the illegal cargo you were carrying.' She had called up an image of the space train and was pointing to the very last car in the long, snaking line. 'A consignment of Cyclo-9 in the compartment nearest the engines. It's volatile and unstable and almost certainly caused that explosion.'

'Then you killed my engineer!' In an act of futility, Guss launched himself at the screen where the president sat, inscrutable. 'You killed Trip Kernow!'

'Where is your proof?' the President scowled.

With the flick of a switch, Anne pulled up another display. Reams of text appeared across the monitor screen.

'This is my proof,' Anne said, simply. 'It was difficult to find but fortunately whoever you paid to hide it wasn't as good at creating encrypted systems as I am at cracking them.' She winked at Jason. 'It's the insurance document from the space train's launch. A fake entry was made in the manifest here.' The text stopped scrolling and a portion of it flashed red. 'Thirty tons of alumina-salts.'

The president hissed from the screen. 'We use them in our building materials. They are very difficult to develop here on Vulcan.'

'Except 30 tons of alumina-salts would have needed a separate export licence which you never applied for.'

The Vulcan was at a loss.

'You never applied for it because you didn't need it.' Anne was moving in for the kill. 'You weren't importing alumina-salts, were you, Mr President?'

The president's mouth was snapping open and shut almost comically, but no sound came.

'Having discovered that, I took the liberty of conducting a multi-band scan of the hole caused by the blast. Here's what I found.' Another image appeared on the screen. It was a chart showing the density of trace elements to be found in the space directly outside the area of the blast. 'Cyclo-9,' said Anne, tapping at the screen where a particular residue was flashing red. 'Outlawed in just about every system in the known galaxy. An intoxicating and deadly drug, unstable in large quantities, smuggled across the galaxy on a train with an ignorant crew.' Satisfied, Anne sat back again, her arms folded across her chest.

Guss was furious. 'You duped us!' he screamed. 'I've worked freight all my life and I've always kept my nose clean. You took advantage of that.' His lip was trembling with emotion. 'You killed Trip Kernow and you would've killed me, too.'

'You couldn't let that ship crash,' Jason said, suddenly understanding. 'There would be an investigation into such a large loss of life. The truth would've come out. So you had to destroy it, no matter who was still on board.'

The president leaned forward, ominously. 'You humans think you're so smart,' he sneered. 'But you're at a disadvantage. I have silos of missiles here on Vulcan pointed directly at you. With your ship gone there will be no record of your findings.'

Anne nodded. 'That would be correct if I hadn't already transmitted my findings to The League of Planets. We're expecting to be joined by their enforcement division any time now. You can save your explanations for them.' Anne smiled, then added a breezy, 'Good luck!'

'Great work, Anne.' Jason leaned over as she switched the screen off. Only now that the president's image disappeared did Anne allow herself to show just how nervous she had felt. She shook her head to clear it.

'Welcome aboard, Mr Guss,' she said, turning to their guest. 'Why don't you get yourself cleaned up and fed before the enforcement division arrives? I'm sure you have a lot to tell them.'

With a weak smile of thanks, Thurlow Guss turned from the flight deck. 'What about your two droids?' He gazed through the cockpit window at his space train, now safely in orbit.

'Oh, they'll both be fine,' Jason assured him. 'We just need to get Alpha hooked up to some juice and he'll be right as rain.'

Guss smiled. 'They're quite a pair.'

Jason nodded and glanced at the scene beyond the cockpit window. Zeta was towing an inert Alpha back to IGR4 from the space train. 'Yup,' he agreed. 'They sure are.'

SECOND CHANCES

'Activate the distress signal!' Vahn's voice cut through the screeching of twisting metal.

'No!' screamed Nev above the din of the alarms. 'We cannot be discovered. How would we explain ourselves?'

Slin twisted 90 degrees in the pilot's chair. 'We won't get to explain ourselves at all if we're dead.'

Nev looked around him. His companions' faces ran with sweat. Their clothes were soaked. Wiping the perspiration from his own brow, he leaned forward to punch at the flight controls. 'Why can't we get power to the engines?'

Slin pointed out the cockpit window. 'That might give you a clue.'

Beyond the glass, Nev could see a wall of molten rock slowly enveloping their craft.

'The external temperature is rising,' barked Vahn as he leaned in close to a monitor. 'Twelve hundred degrees Celsius. The hull's close to buckling with the heat.' He turned to face Nev. 'We need to activate that signal.'

Nev's vision was swimming. He noticed Vahn swaying unsteadily on his feet. Slin was slumping forward over the controls, gasping for air. In just a few minutes they'd be unconscious. And then their vessel would be crushed by the weight of rock. Molten lava would engulf them. Perhaps they'd be discovered in millennia to come, Nev thought morosely, like the ash corpses of Neringa.

'You're the captain,' Vahn was saying. 'The only one who can send that signal.' He clapped his hand on Nev's shoulder, more for support than out of any feeling of companionship. 'We'll think of an explanation,' he gasped. 'Let's live to fight another day.'

Nev breathed hard. The hot air burned his lungs. Vahn was right. He had talked his way out of some serious scrapes before, he felt sure he could do so again. Nev took Vahn's hand from his shoulder and nodded. 'There are no guarantees,' he cautioned. 'We'll be lucky if there's anyone close enough to hear.'

Vahn leaned heavily against a console. 'We'll never know if we don't try.'

'Computer!' Nev shouted over the alarms. 'Activate distress signal, all frequencies! Authorisation, SP-88 oblique two-zero, four-zero.'

The cockpit seemed to swim before him as the computer acknowledged his request. Nev reached out to steady himself as Vahn slipped to the floor. His knees buckling beneath him, the captain fell to the deckplates, his breathing laboured. Just as he slipped into unconsciousness, he wondered if anyone would pick up the signal. And if they did, just what would he tell them?

Anne Warran sat on her bunk, her computer pad on her knees. She thought she would be safer here, away from prying eyes. Intergalactic Rescue 4 was equipped with the most sophisticated communications system The League of Planets could provide, most of it listening for irregular or unexpected signals that might indicate that help was needed. Recently though, she had discovered that the communications array had been secretly reconfigured. During routine maintenance,

Alpha had reported to her that the transmission logs had been compromised. Anne had nodded thoughtfully and made a mental note to look into the matter once she was off shift.

Now she sat, cross legged, trying to take in the full implications of Alpha's discovery. The array had been retuned to make regular sweeps of up to three parsecs from their position. Anne shook her head, her fingers flitting across the keypad. The first sweep had taken place shortly after launch and now they had settled into a regular rhythm: once every 36 hours. The data had been buried beneath the ship's own log transmissions back to The League Headquarters on Earth. Clever. Like hiding a needle in a haystack. But whoever had done it had reckoned without Alpha's superior computing power. Anne switched off her pad and leaned back on her pillow. It had to be Jason, but why? What was he looking for?

A sudden alarm interrupted her thoughts.

'Anne?' came Jason's voice from the comms panel. 'We've got a ship in distress.'

The cockpit was ablaze with flashing lights. Alpha and Zeta stood by the sloping bulkhead wall, ready for their instructions.

'It's coming from the Krona System,' Jason explained as Anne swung herself onto her seat.

'Krona Three, to be precise,' chimed in Alpha, helpfully. Anne noticed the two robots had plugged themselves into the ship's systems.

'Actually, to be *precise*,' added Zeta, 'it's coming from a land mass in the northern hemisphere.'

'Thanks guys,' laughed Anne breezily as she strapped herself in. 'Inhabited?'

'A primitive culture of less than a thousand,' offered Zeta.

'The unstable nature of the environment would make

further settlement difficult,' Alpha concluded with a smug tone.

'Unstable?' Jason swung his seat round, his eyebrows raised.

'The entire planet is subject to extreme tectonic and volcanic activity.'

Jason flashed a smile at Anne. 'Sounds fun,' he winked. 'Let's go!'

In an instant, the ship's Pulse Drive carried Intergalactic Rescue 4 half way across the galaxy, warping space around it as easily as if it were folding paper.

Anne let the air escape between her teeth as she gazed out the cockpit window. The planet beneath them seemed to roll and boil with a restless energy. Sporadic columns of lava spewed from the surface, geysers hissed and bubbled.

'How could anyone live down there?' marvelled Jason, giving voice to Anne's unspoken thoughts.

'I am picking up an abundance of sulphur in the atmosphere,' Alpha reported. 'Plus an awful lot of carbon dioxide, silicon hydroxide and traces of libidium.'

'Libidium?' Jason's jaw hung slack. 'That's the most valuable element in the galaxy.'

Alpha rocked on his feet in an approximation of a robotic nod of agreement. 'There is a concentration of libidium at coordinates zero-five-three by two-seven-five.'

Anne tapped at the monitor before her. 'That's near where the distress signal is coming from,' she said thoughtfully.

'I think it's time we let them know the cavalry's here,' said Jason with a smile and he leaned towards the comms console.

'Unknown vessel,' he began, 'this is Intergalactic Rescue 4 from The League of Planets. What is your emergency?'

He took his finger off the button to await a reply. Nothing. 'Unknown vessel,' he tried again, 'are you receiving us? What is your condition?'

The cockpit was filled with the sound of static.

'Take us in closer, Anne,' Jason commanded. 'Let's see if we can find them.'

Anne reached for the controls. At her command, the rescue craft dropped through the layered clouds of the planet's atmosphere.

'I have isolated the signal,' Alpha announced proudly. Anne was sure she noticed Zeta roll his eyes. 'It's emanating from the active volcano directly below.'

'Someone's in a whole heap of trouble,' Jason muttered, almost too gleefully. 'But how the hell are we going to get them out?'

'It's too hot to get much closer,' Anne agreed. 'Our shields are good but they weren't built to withstand that kind of heat.' She frowned as she thought. 'Zeet,' she turned to the robot by her side. 'Can we get close enough to use the grappler?'

The little droid bleeped. 'We can move close enough,' he said slowly. 'But we can't stay there for long. I'm sending the coordinates to the guidance computer.'

'Oh, come on Zeet, let me take her in manually,' Jason protested. 'I need the practice.'

Anne nodded her assent and Jason beamed in thanks. 'Just be careful,' Anne cautioned. 'You may not get many attempts.'

'Stand by,' said Jason, suddenly serious. Anne felt a rolling movement as the cockpit was buffeted by the thermal winds. The view out of the cockpit window was dominated by the volcano. Streams of lava flowed down its side. Periodically, jets of magma were thrown from its belly into the air. It looked like a scene from Hell. Anne shuddered.

'Okay,' called Jason as a beep came from the guidance console. 'Stand by with the grappler.'

With a curt nod, Anne flicked a switch and a cover slid away to reveal a hole in the flight console. With a hum, a joystick rose into place. A computer monitor flickered into life. As Anne grabbed at the stick, the monitor struggled to display a picture of the scene beneath.

'There.' Anne nodded at the corner of the screen. A cylindrical shape was protruding from the slope of the volcano. Pulling the trigger on the joy stick, she watched on the screen as the grappling line descended. A countdown indicated the length of cable as it unwound from its winch. Anne could see that it was just long enough.

'Hold her steady,' she hissed to Jason. 'Any movement from our current position and I'll miss them.'

'You got it,' Jason nodded as he watched the grappler descend. 'I'll hold her steady as a rock.'

The image on the screen showed the line falling towards the stricken vessel.

'Warning!' Zeta suddenly exclaimed. 'External temperature reaching critical limits.'

'Already?' whistled Jason. 'You'd better be quick.'

Anne was concentrating hard on the image before her. Just as she saw the line reach the desired height from the ground, she pulled on the lever to halt its descent. 'Easy now,' she said, as much to herself as anyone else. 'Easy...'

Anne could feel sweat appearing on her forehead. Squinting into the screen, she manipulated the joystick until the grappler line was in the perfect position. 'I'm activating the magnet.' She threw a switch and felt the joystick shudder as the grappler magnetised. A hum filled the cockpit. 'Hold it Jason, I'm almost there.'

Using her thumb, she pressed a button on the top of the lever. Jason watched on the screen as the grappler's clamps opened like the fingers on a hand. With a deft movement, Anne suddenly pushed the joystick forward and released the button at the same time. The image was clear enough to show the clamps grasping at the stranded ship's engine. With a sudden snatch of the line, the grappler magnetised to the engine's metal components and the clamps contracted to hold it fast.

'Now, Jason!' Anne called. 'Pull up!'

Jason reached for the flight controls, his face a picture of concentration. The entire ship seemed to shake as he engaged the thrusters. Jason grit his teeth as the craft strained against the grappling wire.

'It's shifting!' shouted Anne above the noise, her eyes focused on the screen before her.

'External temperature beyond safe limits,' Zeta reported, a note of worry in his robotic voice.

'Thanks for the update, Zeet!' muttered Jason as he struggled with the controls. The cockpit lurched violently as the ship struggled to lift its load from the volcano. 'It's stuck fast!'

'Let her go,' Anne commanded, suddenly.

'What?' Jason yelled in disbelief.

'Drop her down by a hundred feet. Let the line go slack.' Anne was trying to sound calm. 'Trust me.'

Jason shook his head, resigned. The rising heat in the cockpit was enough to tell him they were running out of time. 'When have I ever done anything else?' he said at last, a broad grin spreading over his face. He leaned forward to disengage the thrusters, and the scant crew felt the ship fall.

'Wait,' muttered Anne, feeling like her heart was in her

mouth. 'Wait…' Blinking sweat from her eyes, she watched the altimeter on her screen clicking down.

'Now!' she screamed. 'Give her all you can!'

Jason didn't need telling twice. Bracing himself against the back of his chair, he pressed hard on the propulsion circuits. With a roar of its thrusters, IGR4 screamed back into the cloud layer, yanking at the grappler line with sufficient force to free the vessel beneath.

'It's clear!' yelled Anne as she pressed a button to lift the grappler back to the ship. The line spooled back onto its winch as Intergalactic Rescue 4 sped away from the volcano's heat.

'External temperature falling,' Zeta reported.

'Zeet,' snapped Anne, 'open the bay doors and lift that ship aboard.'

Zeta beeped in response as Anne unclipped herself from her restraints. 'Coming?' she asked Jason, suddenly much calmer.

Jason nodded enthusiastically. 'Zeet, put the ship in a parking orbit above the rescue site.' He turned as he reached the door. 'Alpha, come with me.'

The sprinkler system had cooled the stricken vessel in the cargo bay, filling the hold with a noxious steam.

'Thank you so much.' Nev, Vahn and Slin stood before the two young pilots, their heads bowed in gratitude. In the bright light of the cargo bay, Anne could see they were of an alien race. They were squat and powerful looking with long arms that reached almost to their ankles.

Nev was doing his best to look contrite. 'Another minute and I don't think we would have made it.'

Jason strolled around the craft. 'Just another day at the

office,' he smiled. The small vessel was bent and buckled out of shape.

'You are both… very young,' Nev said. 'Are you in sole charge of this vessel?' He looked around him for a more senior figure to address.

'Yup,' beamed Anne. 'Just us and the robots. The League of Planets believes the human mind and body is at its most capable between the ages of 17 and 21. So, we're out here for four years, barring visits home, of course.'

'Extraordinary.' Nev's face broke into what Anne presumed to be a smile. Looking closer she could see that the three aliens before her were probably older specimens of their race. Their skin was wrinkled around the mouth and nose and their hair and beards were peppered with grey.

'We can put our droids to work on your ship,' Anne offered at last. 'You're welcome to stay with us in the meantime.'

Nev shared a look with his companions. 'That is most kind,' he said at last. 'But we are eager to get underway.'

'Just what were you doing down there?' Jason had punched a button on a wall screen to call up the schematics of the little craft.

'Geological survey,' said Nev, almost too quickly. Anne noticed the other two crew members were keeping silent, letting their captain take the lead. Was that in deference to his position, or something else? 'The planet below us is unusually active.'

'Well,' said Jason thoughtfully. 'The least you'll need is a new heat shield on this port side. I'll put our droids to work while you freshen up. Alpha here will show you to your guest quarters. They're a little cramped, but they have everything you need.'

Anne caught a look in Jason's eye as she gestured that Nev

and his crew should follow Alpha. 'We'll be sure to have you on your way just as soon as we can.'

Alpha beeped merrily as he limped from the cargo hold, happy to be of service to their new guests.

'What is it?' Anne asked as the aliens left the hold. 'I know that look.'

'Jason,' began Zeta as the two young pilots returned to the cockpit, 'I have taken the liberty of scanning the area around the volcano.'

'Okay,' said Jason as he slumped into his seat. 'What have you got?'

'This.'

With a click, Zeta activated the main screen above the flight deck. It displayed an image from the planet's surface.

'Is that the libidium you mentioned?' Anne leaned forward in her seat to get a better view. A large outcrop of crystalline rock stood, incongruous in the middle of an otherwise barren plain.

'What are those?' Anne pointed to a collection of hunched figures that were approaching the rock.

'The indigenous population,' Zeta explained. 'The League database indicates they are a primitive race, a pre-industrial civilisation.'

Jason's eyes were wide. 'How do they survive in that heat?'

An image of a strange, humanoid creature appeared on the screen. 'They have adapted over the generations,' Zeta chirped, happily. 'An extraordinary example of evolution. They have the ability to tolerate high temperatures.' The creature's internal organs were flashing as he spoke. 'And even go without water for weeks. Their lungs have developed to breathe sulphurous air.'

'What are they doing around that rock?'

Zeta turned to face his master. 'They seem to be worshipping it.'

Jason folded his arms as he turned back into the cockpit. Just as he did so, the three rescued aliens stood at the door. Anne noticed they looked tense as Alpha limped in behind them.

'I hope you're feeling refreshed,' she said, with half an eye on her co-pilot. Jason was clenching his jaw.

'This is quite a ship,' Nev replied, his eyes narrowing.

Anne nodded. 'We like it.'

'There's something puzzling me,' Jason began. Anne could see he was readying himself for a confrontation. The aliens shifted uncomfortably under his gaze.

'I took a look at your vessel while we were in the cargo bay,' Jason continued as he moved towards them.

'Oh?' Nev and his companions looked wary.

'I ran an internal scan to check for damage.'

'And what did you find?' Slin spoke up, his voice thin and reedy.

'Oh, there's damage all right,' Jason admitted. 'Just as you'd expect after what you've been through.'

'Then what seems to be the problem?' Nev met Jason's gaze, defiant.

'It was when I switched to X-Ray that I noticed.'

'Noticed what?' At the end of his long arms, Anne noticed Nev was clenching his fists.

'Nice big cabin,' said Jason, slowly. 'Lots of space.' He turned back to the flight deck and punched a button. The image of the craft's interior was displayed before him. 'If this is a geological survey vessel,' he queried, 'then where are the survey instruments?'

Nev took this as his cue. Launching himself forward, he pinned Jason to the control panel behind him, one hand around his throat. With a roar, Vahn ran at Anne, pushing her away from the controls and towards the door. 'Zeta!' she screamed as she slammed against a bulkhead.

Just as the squat robot turned to offer assistance, the third alien leaped forward. Slin's foot made contact with Alpha's control panel. Suddenly inert, the diminutive robot squeaked in alarm. Small wisps of smoke escaped from his ventilation panels.

'Anne!' croaked Jason, his neck held fast in Nev's grip. 'Disable the controls!' He writhed in pain as he spoke, trying desperately to free himself from Nev's clutches. The alien rolled with him.

'Hold her!' he commanded, and Vahn leaped forward to restrain Anne, holding her head low and her arms behind her back.

Nev grunted as he struggled to hold Jason still. 'Get his legs!' he rasped at Slin. As his companion sprang towards them, Jason kicked out. The force of the movement freed him from Nev's grip and the alien was sent reeling across the flight deck.

'Grab him!' Jason shrieked.

With a deft movement, Anne broke free of her captor and sprang towards Nev. She grabbed at his arm, swinging him to the floor with a scream of defiance. Zeta extended a robotic arm to grab at Slin's leg. The alien fell against the console with a scream of pain, his hand crashing into the controls. The ship gave a sudden lurch and the occupants of the cockpit were thrown against the rear wall. The whine of engines filled the room and the stars blurred through the cockpit window.

'The Pulse Drive!' yelled Jason. 'It's been engaged!'

Anne looked around her. The aliens had ceased their attack. Rubbing at her shoulder, she pulled Jason clear of their assailants. Nev and his crew were shaking their heads. A look of confusion clouded the captain's face. He lifted his hand before his eyes, suddenly studying his fingers intently.

'What's happening?' Jason breathed.

'I don't know.' Anne's eyes were wide with disbelief. Before her, the three aliens were decreasing in size. 'They're shrinking,' she gasped.

'No,' said Jason, 'it's more than that.' He shuffled forward a step. 'They're getting younger.'

Anne could see he was right. The three aliens' clothes were hanging baggily from their shoulders, their arms lost in their sleeves. Darker hair was sprouting on their heads, the lines around their eyes smoothing and fading away.

'Zeet!' Jason shouted. 'Disengage the drive!'

Zeta reached out an arm to connect himself to the flight controls. With a series of bleeps, he tapped into the Pulse Drive. The whining noise subsided and all was quiet in the cockpit.

'What's happened?' Nev was staring at his companions in amazement. Slin and Vahn blinked back, speechless.

'It must be linked to the Pulse Drive,' Anne said warily. 'It happened the moment it was engaged.'

'Zeta?' Jason looked at the droid for an explanation.

A light shone from the robot's visual receptors, bathing the aliens in a probing glare. 'Their DNA has a series of mutations that we do not see in humans.' The light snapped off. 'It has been regenerated in response to an increase in Hubble radiation from the Pulse Drive. In short,' Zeta explained, 'the aging processes have been reversed.'

'How old are they?' Anne breathed, astonished.

'Approximately 15 Earth years,' beeped Zeta. 'Give or take a month or two.'

Jason shook his head to clear his confusion. A more pressing matter was confronting him. Staring out the cockpit window to the stars beyond, he walked back to the control panel and tapped at some buttons. 'Where are we?' he hissed.

'To steady our position for the rescue,' Zeta began, 'I tied the navigation controls to a fixed point in the planet's orbit.' He bleeped happily. 'As the nav controls were still engaged, we have simply returned to our original position. We took a round trip of several light years but we are essentially back where we started.' His visual receptors seemed to wink, mischievously. 'Give or take a mile or two.'

'It's not everyone who gets a second chance in life.'

Jason was leaning back against a food dispenser. The newly repaired Alpha had made his way to assist Zeta with the ship repairs in the cargo bay, leaving the pilot with Anne and the aliens in the canteen. Zahn and Slin were looking sheepish, although Anne noticed that Nev still had a hint of steel behind his young eyes.

'Just think what you can do with all these extra years,' she implored.

'Maybe she's right,' Slin agreed, turning to his fellow aliens.

'You were going to steal the libidium crystal from the planet below, weren't you?'

Slin nodded. 'But we got caught in a lava flow. That rock's worth millions.'

'It's priceless to the people who worship it.' Jason took a sip from his cup. The aliens had been distracted from their attack by the sudden change in their fortunes. He was hoping they would choose to do something positive with it.

'It could make us rich men,' Nev said, quietly. 'If we don't make delivery, it'll cost us dear.'

His companions nodded, fearfully. 'That is true,' confirmed Vahn. 'We have just three days to return with the crystal or we forfeit the deal.'

'What then?' asked Jason.

Nev narrowed his eyes. 'Our lives won't be worth living.'

Jason could tell that Anne was thinking hard.

'What if we gave you a way out of the deal?' she asked.

Slin looked at her. 'What do you have in mind?'

Anne turned to a computer monitor on her table and called up the specs for the alien craft. 'From what I can see,' she began, 'your technology is compatible with ours.'

'So?' Nev looked wary.

'We could fit a small Pulse Drive to your ship. It would be enough to get you far away from here.'

Jason nodded. 'You could start again in another quadrant of the galaxy. Far from the reach of your paymaster.'

'But that's ridiculous,' Nev spluttered. 'I thought you said it was the Pulse Drive that led to this.' He lifted his hands to his face, indicating his new, youthful countenance.

Jason was thinking. 'Zeta said it was excessive Hubble radiation that led to your rejuvenation…'

'If we recalibrated the Drive to absorb more of the radiation,' Anne concluded, following his train of thought, 'it might not have the same effect on your DNA.'

'*Might* not?' Nev looked exasperated.

'We would have our droids run simulations,' Jason assured him. 'To make sure it was completely safe.'

The aliens sat in silence as they considered the offer.

'It would be an opportunity to break free,' Vahn said at last.

'We're young again,' Slin agreed. 'We have a chance to live our lives but this time on the right path.'

They stared expectantly at their commander. Nev sat stock still, his arms folded in thought. 'How far could we go?' he asked at last.

Anne shrugged. 'Anywhere in the galaxy. They would never find you.'

Vahn nodded. 'How long will it take to fit the device?'

Anne looked again at the specifications on her screen. 'I'll get Alpha and Zeta straight on it.' She tapped the table. 'Say, an hour or so?'

Nev smiled. 'Just long enough for you to show us more of this glorious ship.'

As Vahn accompanied Jason to the cargo bay to supervise the refit, Nev and Slin walked the length of IGR4 with Anne.

'If this is Intergalactic Rescue 4,' asked Nev breathlessly, 'does that mean there are three others?'

Anne shook her head. 'Not any more.' They turned a corner. 'The first, Intergalactic Rescue 1, was built as a prototype to test the engines. It had a crew of one human and one droid.'

Slin thought he detected sadness in Anne's voice. 'What became of it?' he asked softly.

Anne stopped and turned to face the two young aliens. 'Nobody knows. They made a last communication in the

Gamma Sector of the galaxy. Near to a black hole. They were never heard from again.'

'I am sorry to hear that,' Slin whispered.

'That's why we have two droids, Alpha and Zeta,' Anne explained as she picked up the pace once more. 'After the loss of IGR1, the League thought having another on board would lower the risk to the human crew.'

'And is that your experience?' Nev asked as he walked beside her.

'Absolutely,' Anne enthused. 'They've definitely got us out of a scrape or two.'

They had just about walked the length of the ship, stopping every now and then as Anne pointed out things of interest. The aliens had marvelled at IGR4's medical facilities and vast array of rescue equipment. Nev had seemed particularly impressed with a hand-held laser cutter. Just as Anne was about to introduce them to the hydroponics suite, a voice came over the internal comms.

'Okay Anne,' barked Jason. 'We're ready.'

Anne turned to her companions just as Nev quickly pushed his hand into a pocket. 'Looks like the tour's over,' she said. 'Let's get to the cargo bay.'

'We've fitted the Pulse Drive and radiation buffer to limit exposure,' Alpha explained proudly.

Jason was waiting for Anne outside the cargo bay doors with Vahn. He nodded thoughtfully as he listened to Alpha's report through the wall-mounted comms.

'I think you'll find *I* fitted the buffer,' interjected Zeta, much to his fellow droid's annoyance. 'And ran several simulations to check it is operating within acceptable parameters.' Zeta bleeped and whirred with what could only be described as smugness.

'I'm pleased to say it is.'

'Okay,' Jason breathed into the comms unit. 'Finish up, you two.'

The two droids retracted their tools and trundled towards the door.

'Then it's safe?' Nev asked, clearly keen to be as sure as possible.

'I can vouch for them,' said Vahn. 'They have both been meticulous.'

Nev turned to Anne. 'It seems your faith in the droids is well placed.'

'Every day,' Anne winked. The two robots chirped with pride as they rolled through the door to join her.

'Have you had a think about where you might go?' Jason leaned against the wall.

Vahn sighed. 'It's a big enough galaxy,' he mused. 'But I've always fancied seeing the Crab Nebula for myself.'

Tapping at a wall mounted screen, Jason pulled up an image of the sprawling interstellar cloud. 'Good choice,' he smiled. 'It's certainly out of the way.'

Slin nodded, enthusiastically. 'We can find somewhere nice and quiet to start again.' His eyes looked suddenly sincere as he held out a hand to the two young pilots before him. 'Thank you for giving us a second chance.'

Anne smiled as she returned the gesture. 'I hope you make the best of it.'

'Good luck out there,' Jason smiled. 'We'll keep an eye on you for a while with our sensors.'

'Oh, I'm sure there'll be no need,' Slin replied, breezily. 'We trust your robots' work. And Nev is a fine captain.' He turned to face his commander, only to see he had gone. 'Nev?'

A sudden hiss told the small party that the door to the cargo bay was closing. 'Nev!'

Jason sprang to the heavy door but it was too late. Punching at the controls on the wall, he peered through the observation window to the cargo bay beyond.

'Nev!' shouted Vahn, putting his shoulder to the door. 'What are you doing?'

Through the glass, he could see Nev slicing at the door controls with a laser cutter. Anne recognised it at once as the one from the equipment store.

A shower of sparks fell from the controls and Nev bounded for his ship. 'You'd better open the bay doors,' he called over the comms, 'or I'll blast straight through them.'

In a matter of moments he was in the cockpit, the ramp to the craft retracting behind him.

'What's he planning?' Anne yelled to Jason.

Her co-pilot turned, breathless. 'Quick,' he panted. 'Let's get to the flight deck. We can monitor him from there.' Vahn and and Slin looked on, helpless, as the two young pilots sprinted from the corridor.

'Zeet!' Jason panted as he swung himself into his pilot's chair. 'Put him up on the screen.'

The small robot was following at speed and, before long, had connected himself to the ship's systems. The screen flickered into life. Below them, the planet's surface was in turmoil. Tectonic plates split apart and lava spewed into the atmosphere. The picture zoomed in on an area in the northern hemisphere and picked out the tribe of indigenous people, gathered around their sacred libidium monument.

'There he is.' Anne pointed to a small craft skirting the contours of a soaring mountain range.

'He is going after the libidium,' said Vahn from the door.

'After everything that has happened.' Slin looked downcast.

'Take us in closer, Zeet.' Anne was struggling with the controls. 'We've got to get him back.' As she spoke, an arc of lava spewed into the air from the volcano below.

'I wouldn't recommend it,' Zeta responded, coolly. 'External temperatures are almost at our tolerances.'

'Nev's craft is equipped with heavy heat shielding,' Vahn explained as he peered at the screen. 'To give us just enough time to grab the libidium.'

'What about the inhabitants? How can they stand all this?' Anne had a look of concern on her face.

'They seem completely unaffected.' Zeta beeped.

'Evolution is a wonderful thing,' Jason hissed.

'He's got it.' Slin was pointing at the image on screen. Following his gaze, Jason could see that Nev's ship had plucked the giant crystal from the planet's surface with an enormous grappler hook. The indigenous creatures were looking on in despair, some throwing flaming rocks in a vain attempt to down the craft.

'Zeet, patch me through to him.'

At Jason's command, Nev's face filled the screen. The young pilot turned to the aliens. Slin stepped forward to make his case.

'Nev,' he pleaded, 'you don't have to do this. We have the tech to go wherever we want. We don't need the libidium.'

'You're weak,' spat Nev from the screen. 'I knew you and Vahn were not of my mind.'

'You're making a big mistake,' Vahn interjected. 'We could all live better lives.'

Nev scoffed from the screen. 'You and Slin can live better lives,' he chuckled. 'I'm going to live a richer one.'

As the crew of IGR4 watched with Slin and Vahn, they could see the crystal being hoisted into position just behind Nev. He turned in his chair to secure the monolith in the holding bay and stowed the grappler hook. The press of a button saw the bay doors close beneath it.

'I must say, I'm grateful to you,' Nev continued as he returned to his seat. 'You gave me back my youth and a means of escape.' He chuckled again. 'I'm not sure what I did to deserve such gifts!'

'We'll find you,' said Anne firmly.

'Oh, I doubt it,' gloated Nev. 'It's a very big galaxy and I have a very small ship.' He raised a hand. Jason could see he was about to bring it down on the Pulse Drive activation button.

'See you around,' Nev sneered, and his hand dropped. The cabin was suddenly full of the sound of struggling engines.

'What's happening?' Anne asked, leaning nearer to the screen. She could see Nev striking the button repeatedly. The engines were whining.

Zeta was busy interpreting the incoming data. 'It's the crystal,' he bleeped. 'It's magnifying the Hubble's radiation from the Pulse Drive causing a shutdown.'

'But what about the buffer?' Slin asked, confused.

'It was never designed to cope with this level of radiation.'

'Nev!' Vahn shouted at the screen, 'Stop! Disconnect the Drive!'

Anne was aghast. 'But if the buffer isn't working…'

Jason caught her train of thought at once. 'His cells will continue to rejuvenate!'

The party watched on in horror as Nev started to shrink before their eyes. Soon he could barely reach the flight deck. Still he pressed down at the activation button, desperate to escape with the libidium.

'He's making it worse!' screamed Anne. 'Every time he tries to activate the Drive, he's getting another dose!'

By now, Nev had realised something was wrong. A look of panic filled his eyes as he grew shorter in stature. Within seconds, he could barely be seen above the flight deck. With its pilot now unable to reach the controls, the small craft gave a lurch and pitched downwards.

'He's going to crash!' Vahn could hardly bear to watch.

Zeta flipped the image to an exterior view. Following the craft's progress on the screen, Anne and Jason watched sadly as the small ship fell out of the air.

'If only he'd listened,' whispered Anne as a plume of smoke appeared from the crash site.

'We do what we can,' soothed Jason, placing an arm around her shoulder. 'But we can't always be responsible for the actions of others.'

With a bleep, Zeta magnified the image on the cockpit screen. The indigenous tribe were approaching the smashed remains of the vehicle.

'They're taking back what is theirs,' said Vahn, agog. As they watched, the creatures – impervious to the heat – were hauling their precious crystal from the wreckage. Boiling lava ran in rivulets around their feet. Once or twice, Anne was sure she saw one of the tribespeople step right into it. They simply carried on with their task, oblivious.

'Let's leave them to it,' she whispered, and the screen went blank. Turning to the aliens by the door, she cast her eyes downward. 'I'm sorry.'

Vahn stepped towards her and took her by the shoulders. 'You have shown us nothing but kindness,' he said. 'Slin and I will be forever grateful.'

Jason sat back in his chair. 'Well, I guess you'll be needing a ride,' he smiled, ruefully.

Leaning over to the navigation controls, he punched in some coordinates. 'Zeet?' he said at last. 'Take us to the Crab Nebula.' He cast his eye over the occupants of the tiny cockpit and could tell they'd need some time to get over this. 'Let's take the scenic route.'

THE SABOTEUR

'Zeet! Have you found it?'

'Negative.'

'Alpha?'

'Negative.'

'Hey,' Jason laughed. 'What's up with your voice, Alpha? You're sounding a little hoarse, there.'

Alpha clicked and beeped as he ran a quick diagnostic. 'All systems are running within acceptable parameters,' he rasped.

'Whatever you say.' Jason puffed out his cheeks in exasperation. On the table before him lay a large jigsaw of a star field, complete except for one last piece.

'I can't believe it,' the young pilot sighed. 'I mean, it's got to be somewhere.'

'That seems logical,' beeped Alpha as he limped back to the table. 'But it's not here.'

'I'm sure it'll turn up,' said Zeta in his most soothing voice.

'Bored?'

Jason spun round to see Anne lounging against the door frame. 'Just filling time,' he shrugged.

'You know,' Anne smiled, 'we've got a whole collection of holo-games.'

'I know,' Jason replied. 'But I'm old school. How's tricks?'

'Oh, fine,' Anne was suddenly serious. 'But I was hoping to talk to you alone.'

Jason looked down at the two robots in the corner. 'Sure. I can leave Alpha and Zeta to look for the last piece of the jigsaw. Let's go to the flight deck.'

'What's the problem?' Jason asked as he sauntered with Anne through the low corridor.

'Alpha found something in the communications log.'

Jason's eyes narrowed. 'What kind of a thing?'

The two pilots swung themselves onto their chairs in the cockpit. Anne thought Jason looked suddenly on guard.

'The communications array has been transmitting regularly since we left Earth.'

'Of course it has,' Jason sat back. 'It's sending data back home all the time. Mission logs, location.'

'But these transmissions weren't *to* Earth.'

Jason was silent.

Anne ploughed on. 'I was wondering if you knew anything about them?'

Jason rubbed his face as he thought. Just as he was about to open his mouth to speak, he was interrupted by an alarm from the communications console. Anne thought he looked almost relieved. Zeta's voice chimed from the speaker.

'We're picking up a distress signal.'

'Patch it through,' Jason barked, almost too quickly.

Anne's frustration at Jason's attitude was replaced at once with a professional interest in the matter at hand.

The screen before them snapped to life. Two images were displayed side by side. One was of an older man with a mane of red hair. He had a low brow and a strong nose. The other image was that of a young woman who, aside from blue hair and softer features, was almost identical in every way. They were both dressed in military uniforms, similar in design except for the colour. The man was dressed in scarlet to match his hair, the woman in a powder blue.

'This transmission has been approved by the Joint Committee of Planetary Emergencies,' declared the young woman in a bold voice.

'The timing, manner and subject matter of our broadcast has been authorised by both races of the planet Binar,' concluded the man.

Anne shared a look with Jason. It was clear they were both reading from a prepared text. Peering closer at the screen, she could also see they were transmitting from different locations.

'We are Anne Warran and Jason Stone aboard The League of Planets' ship, Intergalactic Rescue 4. How can we assist you?'

The young woman chose her words carefully. 'We are in the midst of a global catastrophe.'

'That form of words has not been authorised,' chimed in the alien male on the screen beside her. He seemed to notice Anne and Jason's look of disbelief. 'I will allow *potential* global catastrophe.'

Jason looked bemused. 'We need details if we are going to be of any help.'

The woman with the blue hair began to read from a prepared text. 'The planet Binar is divided into two principal continents,' she intoned, 'Eastasia and Westasia. A joint venture resulted in the building of a power plant where the two continents meet.' She sat back as the man picked up the story, leaning forward to read from a text of his own.

'This power plant is entirely automated.' The picture was replaced with that of a huge structure built on a rocky plain. It was surrounded by smaller buildings and a profusion of pipes that led from its lower reaches into the ground beneath. Its huge dome glistened in the sun.

'It supplies the total power needed by both our continents, provided we use only our allotted half.' There was a tone to the man's words bordering on insinuation. 'An unknown fault has resulted in the reactor going critical.' For the first time, Anne noticed deep emotion in the man's voice. 'Both continents will be affected. Those that survive the initial blast will die within days due to excessive radiation.' His face reappeared on the screen, a downcast expression clouding his already impressive features.

Jason blinked. 'Can't you get in to disable it? Shut the thing down?'

The man shook his head. 'It has initiated its own safety protocols. All entrances have been sealed.'

The female took up the story. 'No one has been inside the building since it was built, four generations ago. It was designed to operate autonomously. Even if we could get in, we would have no idea how to turn it off.'

'How long do we have?' Anne asked, full of dread.

If it were possible, the woman on the screen looked even more serious than before. 'We have just six hours until it blows.'

Anne looked to her co-pilot and raised her eyebrows.

'I am authorised to send you the coordinates of the power plant's location and specifications,' the man concluded. 'If you can help us.'

Anne nodded. 'Send them through,' she said quickly. 'It looks like we have no time to lose.'

As the man leaned forward to flick a switch, the screen went blank.

'I have the coordinates,' Zeta confirmed as he trundled onto the flight deck.

'Punch them in,' Jason commanded as he secured himself with the restraints on his pilot's chair. 'Let's see what we can do.'

Space seemed to split apart. A deep well appeared in the sky above the planet Binar, the light from surrounding stars bending towards it like flotsam around a whirlpool. Then, almost as soon as it had appeared, it vanished, leaving in its wake a long sleek craft bristling with arms and equipment. Intergalactic Rescue 4 had punched a hole from one sector of the galaxy to another. The huge expanse of space between them had been folded and bent into a new shape so that the distance had been traversed in almost an instant.

'There it is!' Anne was craning forward in her seat. On the screen she could see the huge dome of the power plant beneath them. A ream of data scrolled beneath it. 'Those walls are thick,' she sighed as she continued reading. 'If all the entrances are sealed, how on earth are we going to get in?'

Jason had a twinkle in his eye. 'Zeet? You plugged in?'

He looked to where the diminutive robot sat beneath a console, his long mechanical arm snaking across the controls.

'Affirmative,' Zeta bleeped as he plugged himself into an open port. 'Ready when you are.'

Jason sat back in his chair, gripping the armrests in readiness. 'Then employ drill mode!'

Anne's eyes widened in alarm. 'But those systems have yet to be tested!'

Jason smirked. 'No time like the present!'

As Anne sat back in sudden preparation, she sensed movement all around her. The already cramped cockpit was getting smaller still, the walls slowly reconfiguring. Behind her, Zeta whirred and clicked as he accessed the appropriate systems. Through the cockpit window, she saw the nose of the craft divide and retract. There, in its place, whirred a large drill head, its speed increasing as IGR4 angled down to the planet's surface. All along the length of the craft, delicate equipment was hoisted back into the ship's hull for safety. Soon, IGR4 resembled a sleek arrow, the entirety of its outer shell spinning in readiness. A series of manoeuvres found it directly over the power plant.

'Okay, we're going in,' Jason reported, excited. 'Screens only.' Enormous shutters lifted over the cockpit windows. The screens flicked on to show their progress.

'Firing positional thrusters,' Zeta beeped and Anne felt the craft slow. Watching on the screen, she could see they were now just feet away from the dome's surface. 'Contact!'

The cockpit jolted as the drill bit into the thick walls beneath it. Anne marvelled at how Zeta was holding the craft steady while drilling deep into the power plant's outer structure. He fizzed and whirred as he fired thrusters, increased the rate of spin and angled the ship to the position required.

'How's the temperature inside?' Anne asked.

'Tolerable.' Alpha had limped onto the flight deck now.

'How nice of you to join us,' teased Zeta.

'What's up with your voice?' Anne teased.

Alpha ignored her. 'Radiation limits are also within acceptable parameters for humans,' he wheezed, unheeding. 'Providing you suit up.'

Eyeing their progress on the screen, Jason snapped out of his restraints. 'Come on, Anne,' he said, breezily. 'We're almost through.'

'Why is there an increase of Westasian troops along our border?' Commander Kuran's face flushed almost as red as his uniform and hair. He was clearly furious.

'It's merely a precaution,' replied the woman on the screen. She wore the blue uniform of all Westasians.

'Against what?' Kuran spluttered.

'Against your subterfuge.' Commander Saran sat back in her chair and folded her arms.

'That's preposterous,' Kuran scoffed. 'Your energy would be better spent helping to tackle this disaster.'

'A disaster that the Eastasians helped to bring about!'

Kuran looked exasperated at the accusation. 'What on Binar are you talking about, Saran?'

'That reactor was built so that it would never fail.'

'So?' Kuran shrugged.

Saran leaned in close. 'We believe you have been tampering with its systems. The Eastasians are directly responsible for what is happening to that power plant.'

Commander Kuran threw his arms wide. 'And just what will it profit us when our whole continent is reduced to radioactive rubble?'

'Oh, I don't think you're worried about that.' Saran flicked a switch and her face was replaced with another image; a deep hole dug into the sands of the desert. 'Care to explain?'

Kuran bit his lip. 'You realise you've broken just about every treaty we've ever signed by taking that picture?'

'Treaties that were designed to prevent us from learning

the truth about your preparations.' Saran's face filled the screen once more. Her eyes burned with defiance.

'What preparations?' Kuran hissed.

'An escape route for your people. It would be simple enough to evacuate your population underground and wait for the nuclear winter to pass.'

'But that would take decades!' Kuran spluttered. 'Even the Westasians must see how ridiculous that is! If that were the case, show me the live pictures of our population travelling to this supposed shelter.'

Saran swallowed. 'We have no such live pictures,' she admitted. 'But that power plant was built to never fail. How else are we to explain its condition?'

Now it was Kuran's turn to strike. 'That plant was designed to provide power in strictly equal amounts for our two civilisations.' He narrowed his eyes, accusingly. 'The only way it would fail so catastrophically would be if one of us was taking more than their fair share.'

'A baseless accusation!' Saran bellowed from the screen.

Kuran leaned forward to flick a switch. The image changed to that of an enormous industrial complex set into a mountain side.

'How did you get that picture?' came Saran's voice from the speaker.

'It was taken by one of your own generals, Commander Saran. We intercepted his field report to your intelligence command.'

'Thereby infringing every law we have agreed upon!'

Kuran dismissed the picture and Saran's angry face appeared once more.

'Laws that are now declared null and void,' he retorted, 'due to your building of a forbidden launch centre. One that has the capacity to carry your entire population to our moon.' Commander Kuran sneered. 'Just as the planet below erupts into a radioactive ball of fire.'

'This makes no sense,' Saran replied. 'Just how do you think we sabotaged the power plant? Where is your proof?'

Kuran nodded. 'It's true we have no proof, but the building of such an enormous complex would require huge amounts of energy. Perhaps you increased your share of the plant's output, thus bringing about its critical failure.'

'Perhaps?' Saran boomed. 'You build your case on *perhaps*?'

Kuran swallowed. He knew he had nothing more than innuendo to go on. Nevertheless, he must not appear weak. 'In response to your military preparations, I have given orders for an equal and proportionate action. Five of our most heavily armed battalions will face you at the border within the hour.' He clenched his fist. 'If they see any sign of aggression from your troops, they will annihilate your forces.'

He pushed at a button to end the communication. As the screen flicked to black he sat back in his chair, finally allowing his face to wear the expression of horror he had been hiding for the duration of the conversation.

Anne was first off the ramp. With IGR4 having come to rest inside the power plant, both she and Jason had suited up to protect themselves from the radiation. Looking back as she walked, Anne saw the debris and dust left by their ship's progress through the building's outer shell. Above her, a beam of bright sunlight shone through the hole they had made, illuminating the scene around her.

'We've got to head to the main computer room.' Jason's voice filled Anne's helmet. She looked to her co-pilot to see him tapping at a computer pad strapped to his arm. 'It's dead ahead,' he said, pointing the way forward.

'We have a little over five hours,' Zeta cautioned as he trundled behind.

'Plenty of time, Zeet!' Jason yelled playfully over his shoulder.

Ahead of them, a single corridor snaked into the distance.

'Where are all the offices? The control systems?' Jason asked.

'There's no need for them if the whole plant is automated,' Anne reasoned. 'No one was ever supposed to get in here.'

'If no one's supposed to be in here,' said Jason, suddenly alert. 'Then who's that?'

Anne followed his gaze to a bend in the corridor. Just as her eyes focused on a strange figure in the distance, it disappeared around the corner.

'I'm not picking up any life signs at all,' croaked Alpha as he limped down the ramp behind them.

'Well,' breathed Jason as he moved cautiously forward, 'it sure as hell wasn't a mirage. Come on.'

Anne followed in his footsteps, keeping a wary eye out for further signs of the strange figure. Behind them Alpha and Zeta kept their formation, running a series of environmental checks as they brought up the rear.

'The computer room is a hundred metres ahead,' called Jason, tapping at the readout on his computer pad. 'Have you got the plant's specs from Commander Kuran?'

Zeta whirred in response. 'I have, indeed,' he enthused. 'The plans were transmitted to me shortly before we left IGR4. It's an antiquated design, but robust.'

'Then what caused the meltdown?' Anne was treading carefully, her eyes searching the corridor ahead for the intruder.

'Outside interference,' said Zeta, simply. 'It's the only explanation.'

Jason looked thoughtful as he rounded the bend in the corridor. 'Look there!' he gasped.

Anne stepped to one side and peered over his shoulder. Ahead of them stood a large, glass cubicle. Huge cables entered it from above, connecting to a bank of controls within. A column of glowing energy rose from the central console, twisting and writhing as if it were alive.

'The computer room,' she nodded.

'And it looks like our friend is busy at the controls.'

The figure was tall and slight. It wore a tight-fitting jumpsuit and had a smooth, bald head. Its eyes blazed with an inner light and its skin was of a glittering gold.

'I'm still not picking up any life signs,' rasped Alpha.

'But,' spluttered Anne, 'it's right in front of us!'

'It must be mechanical,' mused Jason. 'An android!'

The tall stranger was bending over a console. Suddenly, two fierce beams of light shone from its eyes and raked the computer controls before it. A high-pitched whine filled the air and Anne was sure she felt the ground shaking beneath her feet.

'Er, guys?' said Zeta. 'I may have some bad news.'

'Spit it out, Zeet,' Jason called above the noise. 'What's going on in there?'

'The meltdown has been accelerated.'

Anne shuddered with horror. 'Then how long have we got?'

Zeta clicked again. 'Just 34 minutes.'

Jason clenched his jaw. 'Get me Commander Kuran. Now!'

Kuran was pacing his office. News had reached him of a skirmish with Westasian troops on the border and he was wondering how best to retaliate. He had a good mind to bombard the Westasian's secret launch facility. Perhaps, if they were denied their means of escape, they might work with the Eastasians to neutralise the power plant threat. A sudden buzz from his desk interrupted his thoughts. Striding to his chair, he punched at a button on the comms panel. The wall screen opposite lit up to reveal the face of his adjutant.

'Commander Kuran,' the young man gabbled, 'I have Jason Stone for you from Intergalactic Rescue 4.'

Kuran nodded. With a flick of a switch, the adjutant disappeared to be replaced by the suited pilot in the power plant. Jason was using the camera on his computer pad.

'How are you progressing?' Kuran barked.

'Not as well as we'd hoped,' Jason admitted. 'Take a look for yourself.'

Jason held out his arm so that the commander could see the control room ahead.

'What on Binar is that?' Kuran stepped closer to the screen. He could see a strange figure bending over a bank of computer consoles. Two beams of light were emanating from the creature's eyes. The controls below him sparked and burned beneath the barrage.

'It appears to be some kind of android.' The image zoomed in on the strange figure.

'What's it doing?'

'Sabotaging the power plant,' Jason panted. 'Commander, we have a little over half an hour to fix this. Do you know anything about it?'

'Of course not,' Kuran growled. 'But I bet I know who does.'

Commander Saran sat at her desk playing nervously with a strand of blue hair that had fallen into her eyes. On the computer before her, she could see the build-up of Westasian and Eastasian troops along the border. The two sides were matched, person for person. Even their firepower was of an equal strength. Any confrontation would only result in mutually assured annihilation. All her life, Saran had been trained to hate the enemy, to oppose them wherever possible, to fight them where she could and defeat them whenever there was a chance. Now, she was confronted with another situation entirely. Brinksmanship. It was a question of who was going to blink first. And, beyond all that, they had just hours before the power plant exploded. If those youngsters couldn't save the reactor, then all this posturing along a disputed border would mean nothing anyway. She gnawed at her lip. The idea of the Eastasians avoiding the coming catastrophe alarmed her. On her desk lay an executive order for the destruction of the tunnel system her spies had spotted in the Eastasian desert. Saran sighed. Just as she picked up her pen to sign the order, her wall screen flickered into life. Her comms secretary.

'I'm sorry, Commander,' the secretary said from the screen. 'It's Kuran. He's demanding a final audience.'

Saran raised her eyebrows at the word 'final'.

Kuran's face filled the screen. Saran stood, moving the piece of paper from view as she did so. 'Yes, Commander?'

'Call off the saboteur or face the consequences.'

Though suddenly confused, Saran tried to maintain a neutral expression. 'Saboteur?'

The screen flicked to show images of the strange figure in the power plant. Kuran continued. 'Our rescuers found this creature in the computer room. It is destroying the safety systems that prevent the plant from tipping into critical.' Kuran appeared on the screen again, his arms folded across his chest. 'I do not recognise it as Eastasian, so it must be yours.'

Saran shook her head, perplexed. 'I have never seen it before.'

Kuran slammed his fist down on his desk. 'Lies!' he bellowed. 'Call off the creature or I will deploy missiles against your launch facility.'

'If we register any missiles heading toward Westasian territory,' Saran retaliated, grimly, 'I will destroy your tunnels.'

'Isn't it about time you worked together to save your planet instead of rushing to destroy it?'

The two commanders looked puzzled at the sudden voice. With a flicker of static Anne Warran appeared on the screen. She was shouting to make her voice heard over the rumbling of the power plant's fracturing core. 'We have just 20 minutes to get that android out of the computer room and fix this thing.'

Saran gasped. 'I thought we had hours.'

'Not any more,' warned Anne. Saran could see the building quake around her. 'We need both powers to draw down their energy usage.'

Kuran frowned. 'But that would leave us vulnerable to attack.'

'Not if you both did it together, step by step.'

'You're suggesting we *cooperate* with the Westasians?' Saran almost spat the word.

Anne rolled her eyes. 'You came together to send that distress signal, didn't you?'

'But,' protested Commander Kuran, 'that was in our mutual interest.'

'And so is this.' Anne was clearly losing patience. 'We

need to stem the energy usage from both continents. Only then can Jason and I work on the power systems.'

'And the android?'

'Leave that to us. Now, do it!' With that, Anne disappeared.

Saran and Kuran stared at each other in the ensuing silence, perhaps wondering which of them would blink first.

'They have less than 20 minutes to save the planet,' Kuran said, slowly.

'Perhaps it would be nice,' continued Saran, 'if we had a planet worth saving.'

Inside the power plant, the mayhem was subsiding.

'They're doing it!' Jason shouted with glee. 'They're disconnecting themselves!'

The shrill whining that had threatened to overwhelm them was abating. At last, the young pilots could hear themselves think.

'Alpha, Zeet!' Anne called. 'Stand by!'

The little party watched as the android seemed to sense a change in the power plant's systems.

'With the energy output disconnected, it's going to be caught in a feedback loop.' Jason turned back, looking for shelter.

Anne nodded. 'He's going to absorb everything from the core.'

Jason pulled her into an alcove. It wasn't much, but it would have to do. 'Here's hoping it's more than it can swallow.'

All was suddenly quiet. It felt like the calm before the storm. Alpha and Zeta had positioned themselves just in front of the glass, their visual receptors focused on the android. As they watched, the android's eyes grew large. The searing beams that had emanated from them now seemed to be flowing *into* them. The twisting column of energy above it glowed with a fierce light. With nowhere else to go, the power plant was dumping its excess energy into the android's systems. Circuits and networks stood out beneath its skin like glowing veins. Its body began to strain against the massive amounts of energy flowing into its systems. Soon, it was shaking violently, unable to disconnect itself from the power plant's core. Smoke rose from its golden skin, its eyes burned in their orbits. At last, with a flash, the android was thrown violently back from the console. It smashed through the glass wall to lie, shaking, in the corridor outside.

'Now!' yelled Anne as glittering shards of glass fell all around her.

As Zeta and Alpha sped to the android to restrain it and learn what they could of its origins and intentions, Anne and Jason sprinted to the sparking control panel in the computer room. Its circuits fizzed and popped as Jason waved away the smoke.

'It's taken one hell of a beating!' he called.

Anne was calmer. 'Okay,' she breathed. 'What have we got here?'

Running her fingers over the computer panel in her suit, Anne called up the specs that had been transmitted to Zeta. 'It's a molecular fusion generator,' she said at last. Jason was glad that at least one of them had been listening in their science classes at the Academy. 'Vast amounts of quantum molecular matter are slammed together to create energy,' she continued. 'Clever.'

'But how do we stop it?' Jason yelled over her comms. He was tapping a chronometer on the console. 'We've got 10 minutes!' The energy column was twisting violently as the strain upon it increased.

Anne was thinking hard. 'One of the prerequisites for the success of molecular fusion is the application of heat. The high temperatures that we're seeing are speeding up the process exponentially. Hence the failure.'

'So, what do we do?' Jason was at a loss.

Anne was drumming her fingers on the control panel 'We cool it!' she exclaimed, suddenly.

She looked all around the control unit, trying hard to identify its components. 'There are very few moving parts here,' she said, almost to herself, 'but those that there are will need cooling.' She ran her hands beneath the console. 'Got it!' With an effort, she pulled a length of piping free from the panel. A gaseous vapour spewed from its disconnected end. 'Liquid helium,' she said in triumph. Jason was sure she was almost enjoying herself.

'Now,' Anne continued, 'there must be an output from the core somewhere.' She sprang to her feet once more, her eyes scanning the controls. 'All I have to do is connect this pipe…'

Noticing a thick duct travelling from the centre of the console to the floor, she searched all around it. 'Perfect!' she exclaimed. 'Maintenance hatch!' She turned to Jason. 'I'd cover your eyes, if I were you. Zeet! Alpha! Switch off your visual receptors for 10 seconds!'

Puzzled, Jason turned away and set his visor to block out the light, but not before he read the chronometer and realised they had just four minutes until the power plant blew.

Anne flicked the hatch open. A great torrent of light filled the room as raw energy spewed past the hole in the duct. She shielded her eyes as best she could, but had to focus on pushing the coolant pipe into the energy stream. Feeling with her fingers, she forced the hatch closed again, trapping the pipe in place. Anne's eyes were stinging.

'Jason!' she called. 'I can barely see a thing! It's up to you now.'

Jason cleared his visor and peered carefully into the room. 'What do I do?' He gasped.

Anne propped herself up against the console. 'There's a lever on that panel marked 'extraction'.' She waved in its general direction.

'Got it!' Jason sprung to the lever. 'But if this is a fully automated plant, why does it have controls?'

'How do you think they got it started?' Anne replied in exasperation. 'Now, twist that lever anti-clockwise, past the vertical.'

Jason reached for the lever. 'What will that do?'

'Reverse the extraction process,' Anne yelled. 'It'll cool the core!'

Jason nodded and looked at the chronometer. Two minutes to go. 'Makes sense to me,' he said breezily, and he threw his weight against the lever.

'We don't know how to thank you.'

Commander Kuran stood in his briefing room with Saran, Anne, Jason and the robots, his head bowed in an attitude of contrition.

'Your actions have saved an entire planet.' Commander Saran stood beside him, her eyes upon the two young humans and their droids.

'I'm just glad we were able to help,' replied Anne with a smile. Seeing the two commanders in person, she realised just how much they resembled each other physically.

'This is the first time I have set foot on Eastasian soil,' said Commander Saran. 'That should be some measure of how much we value your assistance.'

'What have you learned about the android?' Kuran asked. Anne noticed him gesture to Saran that she should move before him in the centre of the room. There, on a low metal table, lay the android.

'Zeet?' called Jason as he joined them. 'Why don't you tell them the news?'

'News?' said Saran, her blue eyebrows raised.

'Is it of alien origin?' Kuran looked at the droid for an explanation.

'Far from it,' bleeped Zeta from his position at the foot of the table. 'We have discovered it was created using the same technology as the power plant. At the same time.'

Saran frowned. 'Are you saying the builders of the power plant also built this… *thing*?'

'Then why was it sabotaging the plant's systems?' Kuran was at a loss.

Zeta whirred, happily. 'Perhaps this will help.'

A wall screen behind them flickered into life. They turned to face it as Jason explained. 'Our droids found this video recording in the android's databanks.'

A face filled the screen. It was the face of an older man with soft features. Remarkably, a neat centre parting divided the hair on his head into two colours; red and blue. Saran and Kuran stared at each other, perplexed.

'If you are watching this, then my suspicions are correct.' The man looked sad. 'I am Moran, the builder of your power plant. It was intended to provide power for our planet in perpetuity. As I speak to you, we are a united people. Binar exists beneath a worldwide government, but I sense a change is coming.'

The two commanders watched, open-mouthed.

'The Binarans are splitting into two factions, each

opposed to the other. I foresee a time of division when the two factions will fight against each other, each perfectly balanced, until their mutual destruction.'

Kuran looked guiltily at his fellow commander.

'And so,' Moran continued from the screen, 'I have provided you with a catalyst for peace.'

'The android,' Saran muttered. Anne looked to Jason, pleased that the realisation was dawning.

'The android is designed to monitor planetary communications, like a watchful parent.' Moran smiled at his own analogy. 'If its children become too quarrelsome, it has been programmed to engineer a disaster that will force them to work together for the good of Binar.'

'The meltdown,' said Kuran, his eyes wide in wonderment.

'If you are watching this message, then you are to be congratulated. You have survived a great test and, I hope, learned a valuable lesson.' Moran nodded gravely and, with a sigh, reached forward. The screen snapped to black, leaving the room in silence.

'The tunnels in our desert were not built for evacuation,' said Kuran, at last. 'It is a mine. We have discovered deposits of an ore, resistant to weathering and decay. We are intending to build great cities.' He turned to face Saran, his hand outstretched. 'The Westasians would be happy to share it with our Eastasian cousins.'

Saran brushed her blue hair from her face. 'Our launch facility isn't for escape,' she began. 'We have developed a system for creating medicines in zero gravity. They are stronger and more effective than anything we could create on the planet's surface.' She reached out her hand. 'We would be happy to share them with you.'

As they shook hands, the two commanders turned to smile at their rescuers. Finally, they were the picture of unity.

Jason kicked back in the canteen, pushing his empty plate away from him. 'Here's hoping the Binarans can live together in peace,' he said, smacking sauce from his lips.

Anne was still halfway through her meal. 'They did once,' she said thoughtfully, 'I don't see why they shouldn't again.'

'Perhaps every planet should be given one of those androids,' Jason mused playfully. 'For when things get too heated.'

'Planets?' teased Anne. 'I can think of a few spaceships, too.'

Jason laughed. 'I like to think we can work out our differences on our own.'

A rasping voice interrupted the two pilots.

'Here are the results of our engine diagnostic test, Jason.' Alpha reached out a mechanical hand and dropped a bundle of papers on Jason's lap.

'Oh, great.' Jason's face fell. 'Just what I wanted.'

'You're welcome,' Alpha croaked.

'Hey, Alpha,' exclaimed Jason, suddenly. It seemed something had caught his eye. 'Wait right there a minute.' Reaching out to his plate, he took hold of his fork. Bending down to the droid at his feet, he very carefully teased the prongs into a grating on Alpha's head. The small droid gave a coughing sound as Jason pulled out a small, irregularly shaped piece of cardboard. 'My jigsaw piece!' he laughed.

'It must have fallen from the table in the recreation suite,' Alpha said, his voice suddenly clear as a bell. 'It was lodged in my vocal circuits.'

'Well, you sound much better.' Anne leaned over and patted the small droid.

Jason swung himself from the chair. 'I'm going to finish my jigsaw and then I'll settle down and read these reports.' He held up Alpha's bundle of papers as he left the room. 'Catch you later!'

Anne waved back and settled thoughtfully back into her chair, her mind on her earlier conversation with Jason. She was no nearer to discovering the reasons behind those strange transmissions. Finally, she chuckled at Jason's discovery of his jigsaw piece and shook her head. If only all puzzles were so easily solved.

DOUBLE EXPOSURE

There is no day or night in space, just a never-ending expanse of emptiness, devoid of time. The systems on Intergalactic Rescue 4 had been set to Earth time; that is to say, roughly 14 hours of daylight and 10 of night. Still, there was never complete darkness. Glowing screens and blinking lights meant there was always light of sorts. Even in Anne and Jason's private cabins, there were monitors and computer readouts that pierced the gloom.

On the flight deck, it was usual for Alpha and Zeta to take the night watch. Their human counterparts would be roused if there was any important action to be taken or a rescue to be mounted but, for the most part, it was a matter of monitoring the ship's systems, upgrading components and trying to pass the time.

The night's work done, Zeta had taken it upon himself to teach Alpha a simple card game. They both held a deck of playing cards in their mechanical hands.

'Snap!' called Alpha as Zeta laid down the King of Clubs.

'No,' Zeta reprimanded him, wearily. 'You have to wait until you play your own card before you can call snap.'

'But I know what has gone before,' Alpha pleaded, waving towards the pile of spent cards on the table. 'And I know there is a one in four chance that the card I am about to lay will match yours.'

'Then there is a three in four chance that it won't. The odds aren't in your favour.'

Alpha clicked and whirred. 'I have noticed Master Jason often decides to do things against the odds.'

'That's different,' Zeta snapped. 'He and Anne have something we will never have.'

'What's that?'

Zeta leaned towards his droid companion. 'Intuition,' he said.

Alpha thought for a moment then slammed his card down on the table. 'Snap!' he called again. Zeta's visual sensors grew wide. It was the King of Clubs.

'Perhaps I just got lucky,' Alpha seemed to shrug.

Just as Zeta was about to respond, an alarm sounded from a computer console.

'We're picking up a distress signal,' Alpha announced. 'I'll wake the humans.'

He placed the remaining cards on the table and limped from the flight deck. Zeta watched him go, perplexed. He didn't understand why Alpha didn't want his leg repaired. It would be an easy enough procedure. But then, Zeta mused to himself, there was a lot about Alpha he didn't understand.

Turning to the console, he connected himself to the ship's systems and took a look at the signal.

'It's coming from a rogue moon in the Quadrix System,' Zeta announced as Jason and Anne joined him on the flight deck. They looked refreshed from their sleep but no doubt wished they could have had a little more.

'A rogue moon?' Jason asked, rubbing his face as he flopped into his pilot's chair.

'A moon that's been torn from its planetary orbit due to

collision or catastrophe,' Zeta explained. 'This one is orbiting the Quadrix sun and could once have belonged to any of its 11 planets.'

As he spoke, an image of the Quadrix System appeared on a monitor screen. It showed a large central star and its attendant planets. A small moon flashed at the edge of the screen.

'It's called Janus,' Alpha added as he waddled in behind the human crew. 'After the Roman god of duality.'

'Can we have a closer look?' Anne asked, leaning in towards the screen. The moon grew larger on the monitor and she was able to make out craters and ridges on the surface. 'Is that where the signal's coming from?' She pointed towards a small complex of buildings near the terminator, the area of the moon's surface that fell half in light and half in darkness.

'Affirmative,' Zeta confirmed.

'Then let's go pay a visit.' Jason snapped on his restraints.

'Lay in a course, Zeet,' Anne commanded as she fastened her own seatbelt. 'And open all frequencies the moment we arrive.' Zeta bleeped happily as he tapped into IGR4's navigation controls. A few moments more, and the ship was tearing through a hole in space, reality itself seeming to bend around it.

'Oh, thank God.' The woman on the screen looked relieved. 'You've arrived just in time.'

'Glad to hear it,' Jason beamed. 'I'm Jason Stone of The League of Planets' ship, Intergalactic Rescue 4. What seems to be the problem?'

'I am Zestor, this is my husband, Kelix.' The woman gestured to the man at her side. 'We're both scientists on Janus One, a lunar research outpost.'

'We're here to develop survival techniques for the League's

military division,' Kelix interjected. Jason thought he detected just a hint of annoyance on his wife's face at the interruption. 'We've been conducting a series of lunar exposure tests.'

'Interesting,' mused Anne. 'But why the distress signal?'

'Our life support is down,' Zestor explained, wringing her hands nervously. 'And it's only a matter of time before we enter the lunar night.'

'The temperature will plummet,' Kelix interjected again. 'This far from the Quadrix sun, it can reach minus 200 degrees.'

Jason whistled through his teeth. 'Okay, we'll land on the plain to the south and pick you up with our rover. Then we'll send our droids in to repair your life support.'

'We are indebted to you,' the woman smiled.

'In the meantime, wrap up warm,' added Anne. 'And we'll be sure to have some hot food for you in our canteen.'

Kelix nodded eagerly. 'Most kind,' he smiled. 'Lunar rations can leave a nasty taste in the mouth.' He licked his lips at the thought of something a little more conducive to his palate.

Just as Jason turned to Zeta to offer his instructions, he was interrupted by another alarm.

'Er, Master Stone?' Alpha stuttered from the floor behind him. 'We are picking up another distress signal.'

'I've got it,' Anne said as she leaned forwards to toggle the communications switch.

'Hey!' called Zestor from the screen. 'What's going on?'

Anne offered her most reassuring smile. 'Won't keep you a moment.' She flicked the switch. 'This is Anne Warran of The League of Planets' ship, Intergalactic Rescue 4. How can we assist?'

A burst of static filled the room. Every now and then, Anne could just make out the odd word. It was a man's voice and he sounded desperate,

'Systems failure...' came the voice in between hisses and pops. 'Explosion imminent... need help... rescue...'

The sound cut off and Anne spun round to face Zeta.

'It's coming from the same moon,' the droid explained as he scanned the source of the signal. 'From the other side.'

'What do we do?' Jason gulped.

'We prioritise,' Anne replied, flicking the switch again. The two scientists reappeared on the screen, confused expressions on their faces.

'Is there a problem?' Kelix asked. Anne could see he was already beginning to feel the cold.

'We have a situation on the other side of the moon that needs our attention,' she explained.

'*We* need your attention,' Zestor responded, clutching at her husband's arm.

Anne turned to the diminutive robot beside her. 'Zeet, how long do they have until the temperature poses a threat?'

A quick calculation. 'Two hours,' Zeta bleeped.

'Two hours?' Kelix looked furious. 'We'll be frozen solid by then.'

'No,' Anne soothed. 'You'll be cold, but you'll be alive. And with any luck we'll be back with you way before the two hours are up.'

Jason leaned forward. 'In the meantime, do what you can to keep warm and conserve your energy. You'll be out of there before you know it.'

The two scientists nodded slowly, suddenly unsure if they were to be rescued at all.

'We will come and get you,' Anne said solemnly. 'I give you my word.' The two scientists turned away from the screen and began their search for ways to keep warm in the meantime. Anne switched the image off and turned to her co-pilot. 'You fancy taking us round, Jason?'

'I have control,' Jason smiled, and he reached towards the instrument panel.

There was no discernible difference in the terrain on the other side of the moon, except here it was bathed in the harsh light of the Quadrix sun. Jason had piloted IGR4 expertly around the circumference of the moon, and now the craft hovered above a crater near the equator.

'That's where the signal came from,' Anne reported, 'but it stopped some time ago.'

'Let's hope we're not too late,' Jason said, grimly, as he lowered the craft's nose down towards the moon's surface.

As they descended, Anne spotted the source of the signal through the cockpit window.

'There!' she gasped, pointing through the windshield.

Following her gaze, Jason saw a lunar module standing on a launch pad, steam dissipating from its engines into the vacuum of space. It was a model he recognised from his time at the Academy.

'It's a League Lunar Lander!' he exclaimed. 'They're designed to sit in the belly of the League's exploration craft, then land on planetary moons for observation and experimentation.'

Anne frowned. 'Then surely the two scientists on Janus One must have known about it?'

'Who knows?' Jason shrugged. 'But if the pilot's in danger, we need to get aboard, quick.'

Leaning on the thruster controls, the young pilot brought IGR4 to rest just a few feet away from the module. He winked at Anne as he swung from his chair. 'Let's suit up!' he barked. 'Zeet! Alpha! With us!'

As the two robots trundled from the flight deck in response, Alpha turned to his droid companion. 'I am not convinced that Master Stone has evaluated all the risks.'

'Such as?' bleeped Zeta.

'Atmospheric considerations, terrain issues, security concerns.'

Zeta whistled. 'There is no time to consider everything. A man's life might be at risk.'

Alpha seemed to be thinking hard. 'Then,' he whirred, 'just what is he relying on?'

Zeta's visual sensors twinkled. 'Intuition,' he replied.

As the little party approached the Lander on its launch pad in their spacesuits, Anne was confused.

'It doesn't look like there's any trouble,' she said over the comms.

Ahead of her, Jason agreed. 'There's no apparent sign of an emergency,' he concurred. 'Zeta, how do things look to you?'

'Systems appear normal,' the little robot squawked. 'The engines are stable.'

'Then what exactly is the emergency?' Anne asked herself quietly.

On the nearest side, a ramp led up to a small hatch in the module's hull. Jason bounded up to the door. 'Well,' he panted, 'whoever's in there has made it easy enough to get in.'

'Jason,' Anne called, suddenly suspicious. 'Just be careful.'

Jason beamed his most confident smile. 'It's my middle name,' he winked.

One by one, the boarding party made their way through the hatch and into the Lunar Lander.

Inside, the decor was purely functional. A central living area was surrounded by racks of scientific equipment. A spiral ramp was attached to the outside wall, leading up to a hatch on a higher level, through which the cockpit was situated.

'It all seems a bit too quiet,' Anne whispered. 'Any signs of life?'

Alpha scanned the space around him. 'I'm seeing nothing,' he admitted.

'Then who sent that message?' Jason was heading up the ramp towards the cockpit.

'Perhaps it was automated?' Anne asked, at a loss for an explanation. There was something else bothering her, but she couldn't quite put her finger on it. Jason had reached the top of the spiral ramp and was turning the wheel on the hatch to the cockpit. As he prepared to open the door, Anne suddenly realised what had been bothering her.

'Jason,' she began, 'if the outside hatch was open, then why didn't the pilot just get out of the module if he thought he was in danger? Why bother sending a distress signal?'

At last, the hatch to the cockpit swung open. 'Perhaps he did just that,' Jason called down from the top of the ramp. 'But there's still no sign of an emergency.'

Jason heaved himself up through the hatch and found himself in the middle of the Lunar Lander's cockpit. All was quiet. The gentle hum of the module's background systems was accompanied by the twinkling of lights from banks of switches and dials. Two pilots' chairs sat empty before a dashboard, the cockpit windscreen staring up into the silence of space. Jason frowned. As far as he could tell from the various readouts and monitors, the module was operating smoothly. There was certainly no sign of anything that might have resulted in a distress signal being sent.

'There's nothing up here,' he called down through the hatch, only to be met with a stony silence. 'Anne?'

'Er, Jason?' came Anne's plaintive response at last. 'I think you'd better get down here.'

The young pilot swung himself back down through the hatch and stood at the top of the ramp. Looking down into the main body of the craft, he found himself faced with the barrel of a laser rifle. 'Hey!' he yelled in surprise. 'What's going on?'

Below him, a man was standing in a spacesuit, his visor flicked up to show his face. His hairline was just visible beneath his helmet, and Jason noticed grey at his temples. He was standing immediately behind Anne, with two rifles in his hand. One, he had trained on the young woman before him, the other on Jason. What could be seen of the man's face was lined with sweat, and Jason could see his steel blue eyes were twitching feverishly.

'Come down,' the man rasped, keeping his weapons levelled at the two young pilots. 'And keep your hands in the air.'

'None of us are armed,' Jason said as he walked gingerly down the ramp.

'I'm not taking any chances,' the stranger replied, his mouth twitching as he spoke. 'I want both of you to back off slowly towards that computer bank. The robots, too.'

Jason joined Anne and the droids as commanded.

'What do you want from us?' Anne asked, carefully.

'Nothing.' The man looked angry. 'I want you to do *nothing*. Stay here and do *nothing*.'

'We received a distress signal from this vehicle,' Jason said. 'We're from The League of Planets. Our rescue craft is parked just outside and is at your disposal.'

'What seems to be the problem?' Anne asked, anxiously.

'Oh, no problem,' the man laughed. Suddenly, his whole demeanour had changed. 'No problem at all!' Then, just as suddenly, his mood darkened again. 'Yes,' he hissed, tightening his grip on his laser rifles. '*They're* the problem.'

Jason blinked. 'Who?' He could only think he meant Zestor and Kelix. 'The scientists?'

'Scientists?' the man bellowed. 'Amateurs, more like.'

Anne shared a look with Jason. The man seemed desperately unstable. 'We need to get back to them,' she explained. 'We've got an hour until night falls on their base.

'Let them freeze!' The man was shaking now, his eyes bulging in their sockets.

'Hey,' soothed Jason. 'Why don't we all just calm down.' He was thinking fast. 'If it's us you want, then fine. But why not let our robots go to rescue the scientists?'

'If those tin cans so much as make a move for the door, I'll blast you all to kingdom come!' The stranger was swinging his guns around him wildly as he spoke. Anne was sure he was going to open fire.

'Surely you don't want their deaths on your conscience?' she asked.

The man threw his head back and laughed. 'Who says I have a conscience?' he roared. 'Why should they take credit for my discoveries? I say *let them die.*' He was backing away towards the door now, his eyes flicking nervously around the room.

'What of us?' implored Anne. She could see the man was about to make a swift exit.

'Who cares?' came the answer. 'It'll be night time soon enough and I'll be on my way home to the glory I deserve. Why should I care what becomes of you? You're just a couple of kids.'

With that, he threw himself through the door and slammed it shut behind him. Jason ran to it at once to find it jammed. He heard the sound of laser fire.

'He's disabled the mechanism,' Jason breathed, despondent.

'Who was that man?' Anne relaxed now he was gone. 'Zeet, did you get a good look at him?'

'I certainly did,' Zeta bleeped, encouragingly. 'I'm just running his details against the League's database.' A long arm snaked out from his squat body and soon he was connected to the Lunar Lander's systems. A monitor near a bank of computers flickered into life. 'Searching.'

While a picture of the man in his space suit occupied the left-hand side of the screen, just as Zeta had seen him, a series of images scrolled across the right-hand side. Having fed the physical details of the stranger into the database, the little droid was trying to find the closest fit.

'That's him!' exclaimed Anne, at last. 'I recognise that face.' The scrolling images had come to rest on the face of a middle-aged man, greying at the temples but with steely blue eyes.

'Facial and bone structure are a match,' Zeta agreed. 'As are height, estimated weight and build.'

'Then he's our man,' Jason said excitedly. 'But, who is he?'

'Harlen Godrick,' Zeta replied.

Anne blinked. 'I know that name.'

'Godrick is known on Earth as a space survivalist,' Zeta continued. 'His experiments in hostile environments have greatly expanded human knowledge of endurance and the body's capacity to withstand extremes.' A list of awards and honours scrolled across the bottom of the screen. 'As a result, he has been awarded The League Medal, a Presidential Award, The Galactic Hero Award and a Golden Comet for Services to Science.'

'I remember now,' Anne interjected. 'He must have risked his life a dozen times. I watched a vid report on his deep space walk.'

'So, he's a hero,' Jason whistled.

'He didn't *seem* like much of a hero a few moments ago,' Anne scoffed. 'What's he doing on Janus?'

Zeta clicked and whirred as he searched the database for more information. 'Latest records indicate he was part of a three-person expedition to monitor the effects of isolation and solar radiation on the human body.'

'Solar radiation?' Jason raised his eyebrows. 'Sounds fun.' He gave a wry smile.

'So he came out here with Zestor and Kelix.' Anne looked thoughtful. 'Why didn't they mention him?'

'From what I saw,' suggested Jason, 'there's no love lost between them. But I guess only they can tell us why.'

'We need to get to them, and quick,' Anne said, suddenly. 'We can't let them freeze out here.'

'Master Stone,' bleeped Alpha from the floor at the young pilot's feet. 'I'm receiving a situation report from IGR4.'

'Why?' Jason asked. 'What's up?'

'Vertical thrusters have been engaged.'

'What?!' Anne spun round to look through a porthole in the module's side. Sure enough, she could see Intergalactic Rescue 4 lifting off from the surface, kicking dust and debris into the moon's thin atmosphere. 'He got on board!'

Jason looked suddenly guilty. 'I didn't think there was any reason to engage the security systems.'

'Of course not,' Anne smiled. 'We're on a barren moon a billion light years from Galactic Centre. Why should you lock the door?'

They watched as the ship lifted gracefully into the air and disappeared behind a ridge. 'Where's he going?' Jason wondered aloud.

'I don't know,' admitted Anne, 'but right now our priority has got to be to rescue those two scientists from Janus One.'

'But how?' Jason looked defeated. 'With IGR4 gone, what can we do?'

Anne was already making her way up the spiral walkway to the cockpit hatch. 'We improvise! Zeta, Alpha, I need you.'

Poking her head through the hatch to the cockpit, Anne saw a compact but tidy space lined with computers. Sitting gingerly in the pilot's chair, she took a moment to familiarise herself with the controls. Luckily, there was nothing there that she didn't recognise to some degree. As this was a League of Planets craft, the navigation, propulsion and flight controls were all of a design that she had experienced before.

'Zeet,' she began as she strapped herself in. 'Get in touch with Janus One and tell the two scientists we're on our way back to get them.'

'What about Godrick?' Jason had joined them in the cockpit and was looking through the windshield. He could just make out the glare of IGR4's engines in the dark sky. 'We can't let him get away with our ship!'

'Leave that to me,' bleeped Alpha unexpectedly.

'Okay,' Anne smiled as Jason secured himself for take off. 'Godrick might think we're just a couple of kids, but he made one big mistake.'

'What's that?' Jason asked.

'He underestimated us.'

The Lunar Lander lifted off gracefully from the moon's surface. It took no time at all for Anne to gain mastery of the controls. Soon, they were skimming across the craters and over fissures, rising and falling with the contours of the landscape.

'I have Zestor and Kelix on screen,' Zeta said.

'Put them up,' replied Jason, archly. 'Let's see what they've got to say for themselves.'

A small screen flickered into life and the two scientists appeared, side by side. They had scrambled into their regulation space suits in anticipation of their rescue, but Anne could see they were still shivering with cold.

'Hang on in there,' she encouraged them. 'We're just minutes away.'

'Please,' begged Kelix, 'be as quick as you can.'

Worryingly, Anne could see the condensation inside his visor beginning to freeze.

'Oh,' interrupted Jason breezily, 'while we were out here, we ran into an old friend of yours.'

There was an uneasy silence as the two scientists shared a guilty look.

Jason pressed on. 'Why didn't you tell us about Godrick?'

Zestor cleared her throat. 'We had no idea if he was still alive or not.'

'Oh, he's alive alright,' Jason hissed. 'Alive enough to point a gun at us and leave us stranded in this module. It's lucky for you we know how to fly it, or you'd have our deaths on your conscience too.'

'Godrick is not on our conscience,' Zestor insisted. She was stamping her feet in a vain attempt to keep warm.

'He was half crazy before he even came out here.' Kelix looked furious. 'The League humours him because he's a hero, but they should stand up to him. The man's a danger to us all.'

Jason was suddenly interested. 'What happened?'

Zestor swallowed. Her teeth were beginning to chatter as she spoke. 'His survival experiments were becoming ever more extreme.'

Kelix nodded. 'It was all we could do to stop him going out on the surface without his suit.'

Shooting him a look of annoyance, Zestor continued. 'His exposure over the years has affected his brain. He was already showing signs of paranoia when he arrived here. He was certain The League was out to discredit him and strip him of his honours. It was all unfounded, of course.' Zestor was shivering now. 'Soon, he suspected we were in on it. He grew more certain that we were out to sabotage his experiments.'

'We confronted him,' Kelix interjected, clearly concerned at how cold his wife was suddenly feeling. 'We tried to make him see sense, to show him that we're all working for the same side but he wouldn't listen. Finally, he convinced himself that we wanted to take credit for his work, so he sabotaged the base's life support and commandeered the Lunar Module.'

'He left us to die!' Zestor could no longer keep a hold on her emotions.

'Nobody's going to die,' Anne replied as the lights snapped on in the cockpit. 'We've just crossed over the terminator, into the moon's night. We'll be with you shortly. If anything, Godrick has done us a favour. We could never have got so close in IGR4.' She eased the flight controls down towards the base. 'I'm going to be able to park right outside your front door.'

Kelix was looking down at a screen. 'We see you!' he confirmed. 'Come on Zestor, dear. Time to get out of here.' Their image faded as the two scientists shuffled away, faces shivering with cold behind their visors.

Reaching up to the propulsion controls, Anne angled the aft thrusters to bring the module down with a soft bump.

'Just in time,' she said with relief. 'Jason, you want to go and let them in?'

'Sure,' Jason beamed. He stopped at the cockpit hatch. 'But then what? This thing has no range at all. How are we going to get back to IGR4?'

Anne shrugged. 'Alpha says he's on it,' she said, gesturing to where the small droid sat crouched on the floor, beeping quietly. 'So let's leave him to it!'

With the module safely landed just feet away from the base, it was an easy matter to guide the two scientists over the short expanse of rocky terrain and into the warmth of the Lander's living quarters.

'Just how long have you been out here?' Anne asked as she offered them hot drinks from the dispenser.

'Three years,' replied Zestor, wriggling her fingers in the warm air. 'It's a deep space mission so The League decided to send a married couple.'

'This far from Earth,' Kelix joked, 'no one can hear us arguing!'

'Godrick joined us a year into the mission, and brought some unorthodox methods with him.' Zestor took a drink from her cup. 'Instead of testing the effects of solar radiation on our cultivated bacteria, he would insist on testing them on himself.'

'He would lock himself on our observation deck and

deactivate the radiation shields.' Kelix shivered again but, this time, not from the cold. 'We would hear his screams.'

'At last, he went completely mad,' Zestor concluded. 'He disappeared two days ago and we haven't heard from him since. We assumed the worst.'

'You waited two days before sending your distress signal?' Jason sat beside them.

'I'm an engineer by training,' Kelix muttered. 'I thought I could fix the life support, but I didn't have the know-how.'

'I'm still very proud of you,' said Zestor quietly. 'And look,' she gestured around her. 'All's well that ends well.'

'Not quite,' said Jason, standing up suddenly. 'What are we going to do about Intergalactic Rescue 4?'

'Master Stone,' came Alpha's voice from the top of the spiral ramp. 'Perhaps you would like to join me in the cockpit?'

Casting a look to Anne, Jason sprinted up the ramp, his co-pilot following just a few steps behind.

Stepping through the hatch, he was greeted by the sight of a large ship looming into view through the Lunar Lander's window.

'IGR4!' exclaimed Anne as she leaned against the flight deck. 'But how?'

'I took the liberty of engaging the Emergency Recall Device,' Alpha bleeped, proudly. 'IGR4 was instructed to home in on our position and return as quickly as possible.'

'I didn't know we even *had* an Emergency Recall Device,' laughed Jason as he patted Alpha's head.

'We didn't,' the little robot whirred, 'until last night. I fitted the component myself as part of my routine maintenance and upgrading programme.'

Anne was amazed. 'But how did you know we would need it just hours later?'

In response, Alpha shuffled round to Zeta and winked his visual circuits. 'Let's just say it was intuition,' he bleeped.

Harlen Godrick lay on the medical bed, a monitor beside him showing the progress of the procedure. As soon as Intergalactic Rescue 4 had landed, Anne, Jason and the two robots stormed the ship to apprehend the hijacker. Godrick had made little resistance. With the ship returning to Janus One, he had clearly realised the game was up. Just as Jason had relieved him of his weapons, Godrick had fainted. After a brief period of fits, he had laid stock still, his eyes staring sightless at the ceiling. With the help of the two robots, Anne had rolled him onto a stretcher and conveyed him to the ship's medbay.

'How's he doing?' asked Jason as he led the two scientists to Godrick's bedside.

'Ask him yourself,' Anne smiled. 'He's just coming round.'

Godrick opened his eyes slowly to focus on Zestor and Kelix. Zestor reached out a hand to stroke his hair.

'Zestor?' Godrick croaked, his throat dry. 'Where am I?'

Kelix leaned forward to explain. 'This is Intergalactic Rescue 4, a League ship. These two young people are its crew.' He looked around. 'And what a marvellous ship it is, too.'

'How did I get here?' Godrick propped himself up on his elbows to look the two young pilots up and down.

'You really have no memory of the past few hours?' Jason asked.

Godrick shook his head. 'Last thing I remember is working on the vacuum experiments with Kelix.'

Kelix's eyes grew wide. 'But that was three weeks ago.'

'It might be a side effect of your treatment,' Anne began, thoughtfully, looking at the readout on the monitor.

'Treatment?' As if for the first time, Godrick noticed the line of clear fluid attached to his arm. He had a look of panic in his eyes.

'You've been very ill,' Zestor smiled. 'For a long time.'

'We've given you something for radiation poisoning,' Anne explained. 'You might have some short-term memory loss as a result.'

'What about our experiments?' Godrick asked, suddenly concerned.

'They can wait for now,' replied Kelix. 'We need to get Janus One back up and running first.'

'Why?' Godrick looked confused, as if groping for a long-forgotten memory. 'What happened?'

Just as Kelix was about to explain, Zestor rested a hand on his arm and shook her head gently. 'There was an accident,' she smiled. 'Nothing to worry about. I'm sure our hosts will be only too happy to help fix things up before they leave.'

Just as Jason opened his mouth to protest, Anne jumped in.

'Of course.'

'But,' Jason began.

'Jason,' Anne chided, 'some things are better left in the past.'

Jason was about to respond when he saw a certain look in Anne's eye. It was a look he had grown very familiar with over the preceding months. It was a look that said her mind was made up, and there was no point in trying to get her to change it. Jason sighed as Anne led him away to the door.

'We won't be entering this particular rescue into the log

book,' she whispered. 'Godrick has given so much to society.' She turned to see Godrick chatting amiably with his two scientist friends. 'And, if Zestor and Kelix are willing to forgive him,' she concluded, 'then perhaps we should, too.'

THE TROGLODYTES

'It's an observation mission?' Jason was incensed. 'We've got a ship full to the brim of state-of-the-art rescue equipment, and they're sending us on an observation mission!'

The young man bit down miserably on his sandwich. Even the taste of the cheese inside it annoyed him.

Pulling up a chair next to her friend, Anne tried her best to placate him. 'We can't always be zooming around the galaxy,' she said. 'Sometimes the most mundane tasks are the most important.'

'But never the most exciting,' Jason sighed. 'What could be so important about watching a primitive planet?'

'It's an opportunity to contribute to the sum of human knowledge,' Anne winked at him. If truth be told, she knew exactly how he felt. But, if the odd scientific mission was the price to be paid for a life of adventure, then so be it.

'I'd rather contribute to the sum of Jason Stone's excitement,' Jason sneered.

'Who knows?' Anne teased. 'You might be surprised.' She poured a cup of coffee and sat back in her chair. 'And if you find something really important, they might name it after you.'

Jason waved absently at the screen on the wall. It showed a large planet revolving beneath them. 'What could there possibly be to discover down there?' he snarled, dismissively. 'It's just a mudball.'

Just as Anne was about to respond, Alpha's voice cut through the comms system.

'Ms Warran,' he chirped, 'analysis complete.'

'What's that?' Jason asked.

Anne swallowed. 'I asked Alpha to run a diagnostic test on the Pulse Drive.' She hoped it wasn't obvious she was lying. 'I was just wondering if we could increase its efficiency.'

Anne found the little droid in the computer control room. Situated at the heart of the ship, it was the centre for all of Intergalactic Rescue 4's systems. The walls comprised great banks of computers, their fans whirring, indicator lights blinking feverishly. A central console provided continuous feedback on all the ship's processes. Alpha was squatting in an alcove, his mechanical arm plugged into a computer interface.

Anne took a look back up the corridor before shutting the door behind her. She wondered if Jason was at all suspicious of her behaviour.

'What have you got, Alpha?' she asked quietly, bending down to the little robot.

'I have analysed all transmissions from the communications array, as requested,' he bleeped, 'and I believe I have detected a correlation between the array sweep and the locations of recent missions.'

Anne frowned. 'What do you mean?'

A nearby screen flickered into life in response. 'This is a representation of recent missions mapped against our quadrant of the galaxy.'

Anne stood up to peer closer at the monitor. It showed a point at the bottom left-hand side of the screen labelled IGR4.

Dotted around the screen, Anne saw various star systems and planets ringed and tagged with their mission labels. She recognised them at once as being the sites of recent rescue missions; the Quadrix system, the planet Vulcan, Krona Three.

'What exactly are you showing me, Alpha?' Anne narrowed her eyes in thought.

'This is the area covered by the anomalous transmissions.' On the monitor, Alpha superimposed a coloured band emanating from IGR4. With a start, Anne realised it encompassed the sites of their recent rescues.

'Does this mean what I think it means?' she asked, hardly daring to consider the implications.

'It means,' began Alpha, patiently, 'that we have only been responding to distress signals within the same area covered by the outgoing transmissions.'

Anne was thinking fast. 'It's a deliberate attempt to guide our trajectory in a particular direction.'

'Far from being random as you might expect,' Alpha concurred, 'we have only been answering distress signals within a particular area of space.'

Anne's eyes were wide in disbelief. 'Using the coordinates we have from previous missions, can you extrapolate our ultimate destination?' She was at a loss to explain just what Jason had been up to.

Alpha whirred and clicked as he applied himself to the calculation. 'I cannot be specific without further data,' he said, at last. 'But our ultimate destination is somewhere in the third quadrant.'

Anne shook her head. What on Earth could this mean? Just why was Jason sending covert transmissions into space? And why was IGR4 only responding to distress calls that matched his intended trajectory? 'He's trying to cover his tracks,' she whispered to herself, suddenly alarmed.

'Everything okay here?'

Anne wheeled round as the door hissed open. Jason stood in the corridor. She hoped she was hiding the monitor from view with her body.

'Sure,' she said, reaching behind her to switch the screen off. Had he seen anything? 'I think we may have increased efficiency by 15 per cent.'

Jason nodded. 'You've been busy,' he said with a smile that was impossible to read. Anne wasn't sure what to say. 'Anyway,' Jason continued after an awkward pause, 'we've got our orders from Earth Control. Wanna come take a look?'

'Sure.' Trying to appear as casual as possible, Anne turned to her robot companion. 'Good work, Alpha. We'll finish up here later.' She patted the droid on its head as Jason turned away from the door. With a final look around the computer control room to be sure she had left nothing incriminating behind, Anne sighed with relief and followed her co-pilot to the flight deck.

The Science Chief had a formidable appearance. Jet-black hair was swept back from a heavy brow. A square jaw and impressive nose loomed from the screen.

'Tritan Four is a billion years into its evolution,' he was saying. 'We'd like Intergalactic Rescue 4 to monitor the planet for any signs of life.' The chief had a voice as impressive as his appearance, low and sonorous. 'We can then compare them with those believed to have existed on Earth at a similar stage of its development. The question is this; does all life evolve at the same rate?'

'Sounds fascinating,' remarked Jason, clearly unimpressed.

'We're good to go,' Anne interjected, cheerfully. 'Aren't we Jason?'

'Sure,' Jason agreed. 'Ready as can be.'

The Science Chief nodded. 'Then we'll expect your report in 48 hours.' He leaned forward to end his transmission and the screen went blank.

'Forty-eight hours?' Jason hissed.

'Time flies when you're having fun,' Anne teased. She wondered why he was so unhappy at spending time in one place. He was clearly in a hurry to get somewhere.

'You want to take her down?'

Cheered by the prospect of taking the controls, Jason smiled suddenly. 'Sure!'

As the ship descended through the cloud layer, Alpha and Zeta joined their human companions on the flight deck, each plugging themselves into their relevant interfaces.

'I'm logging microbial activity in the atmosphere,' Zeta reported. 'Simple bacteria trapped in the moisture.'

'Sounds promising,' Anne nodded. 'Take her in lower, Jason. Let's scan the planet's surface.'

Concentrating hard, Jason activated the thrusters to keep the ship at a stable distance from the terrain below. Looking through the windshield, he saw impressive valleys threaded between high peaks of shining rocky mountains.

'They contain deposits of quartz and mica,' Alpha bleeped.

Anne looked up. 'That's why they're gleaming in the sun,' she smiled. 'Pretty.'

Jason was leaning on the thruster controls now, bringing the craft down in a secluded glade. With a hiss of hydraulics, it came to rest on the soft, muddy ground.

Zeta seemed to jump. 'Ms Warran,' he began. 'I'm picking something up on the audio sensors. It seems to be coming from beneath the planet's surface.'

The cockpit fell silent as Jason cut off the engines.

'Let's hear it,' Anne commanded.

Zeta beeped as he played the sound over the comms. At first it was muted, as if heard from underwater.

'Can you clean it up at all?' Anne was listening hard.

Zeta clicked as he sharpened the signal. Finally, through a hiss of background noise, came an unmistakable sound; a rhythmic double thump.

'That sounds like a heartbeat!' Jason exclaimed from his pilot's seat. 'Can you pinpoint its location?'

Zeta placed a map of the local terrain on a screen. With each passing heartbeat, he zoomed in on an area of scrubland to the south, eventually settling on a subterranean cave system viewed in infrared. 'There,' he chirped. 'Just a quarter of a kilometre away.'

'I guess we need to verify our findings,' beamed Jason, already halfway out the door. 'Time to suit up?'

Anne smiled at the difference in her co-pilot now there was some investigating to be done. 'Time to suit up,' she agreed.

As they both left the flightdeck, Zeta called them back. 'Wait!'

'What is it, Zeet?' Jason panted, reappearing at the door.

Zeta increased the volume from the audio sensors. The single heartbeat had been joined by another, then another. Soon it was a cacophony of competing drum beats.

'Sounds like one hell of a welcoming committee,' Jason beamed with excitement. And, with that, he was gone.

The mouth to the cave system was shrouded in fog. Leaving the droids in IGR4, Jason and Anne picked their way between clumps of strange grass and large-leafed plants. The atmosphere was damp and acidic so they had donned lightweight breathing apparatus. With just a single backpack containing equipment and supplies between them, the going was quick. The moisture in the air condensed on their skin as they strode through the foliage, giving their faces and hands a lustrous sheen. The entrance to the caves was through a thin crack between two great crags of rock. Reaching for their torches from the backpack, the two friends descended into the darkness.

'Have you noticed something, Jason?' Anne was looking around carefully as she walked. Jason flashed his torch along the sheer rock.

'It's dark?' he teased.

'It's dry down here. No sign of water at all.'

Jason saw that she was right. Just about every cave he had ever been down had been running with water, but these walls were as dry as a bone.

On and on they walked, with no sign of life to be found. 'You getting all this, Zeet?' Anne asked into her computer pad.

'Affirmative,' came the response.

'Are you sure we're heading in the right direction?'

'Affirmative. You are only a few metres away on a lateral plane, but you have quite some way to go down.'

'Okay,' sighed Anne, 'let's keep comms open in case we need help.'

Sure enough, the way ahead was steep. More than once, the intrepid explorers lost their footing and had to reach out to steady themselves.

A soft beeping sound came from Anne's wrist mounted computer pad and she looked down to read the notification.

'Hey!' she exclaimed. 'The air down here is oxygen rich. Breathable.' She slipped the breathing apparatus from her face and took grateful lungs full of sweet air.

'Must be chemicals in the rock,' suggested Jason as he removed his own breathing mask. 'Neutralising the acid, somehow.'

After a short break to catch their breath, the two friends pressed on. Sometimes they had to crawl on their bellies to traverse from one section of the cave system to another. Other times, they found themselves climbing down near vertical shafts. At last, they found themselves on level ground and the two companions stopped for breath.

'Listen,' said Anne suddenly as the sound of blood rushing in her ears subsided. Jason held his breath to hear. From a turning just ahead, he could hear the sound of people murmuring. As he concentrated, the sound seemed to solidify into a melody, deep and solemn.

Anne held her finger to her lips to signify they should proceed with caution. They stepped gingerly round the corner to see what could be seen.

They stopped mid-stride as the spectacle presented itself to them. A large group of people were swaying before a rock monolith, their hands held up in supplication. The rock was bathed in a single shaft of light that penetrated through a crack in the rock above. The minerals in the rock shone and sparkled in the light, reflecting strange shapes onto the cavern walls. The creatures' wide eyes looked up to the light source as they sang in unison. Although they were clearly naked, their bodies were almost entirely covered with long, matted hair. Suddenly, an animal scream pierced the air. Anne and Jason had been spotted.

'There are Unknowns among us!' came a cry, and soon the word was repeated by the strange congregation. 'Unknowns! Unknowns!'

The two friends pressed themselves against the rock as the crowd advanced.

'We're your friends!' Anne shouted above the din, more in hope than expectation. Surprisingly, the crowd stopped. Expressions of confusion clouded their eyes.

'You speak our language,' said the lead alien in wonder. The hair that covered his body was streaked with grey and he carried a gnarled staff.

Jason turned to his companion, his eyebrows raised.

'It's the ship's translator,' Anne tapped the computer pad on her wrist. 'There's obviously something in the language it recognises.'

'Makes sense, I suppose,' Jason nodded. 'If these creatures are on the same evolutionary path as humans, then perhaps our languages share a common root.'

The first alien was leaning in towards Jason, a long finger outstretched to his face. 'What is... *human*?' he whispered in awe.

'*We* are human,' Anne said, bravely. She took a step forward and spread her hands wide to show she posed no threat. 'I am Anne, this is Jason.'

The congregation before them took up their names as a chant and the words echoed around the rock cathedral.

'I am Novar,' the alien announced. 'High Priest of the Rock.'

Jason nodded over his shoulder to the edifice in the centre of the cave. 'And I suppose that's the rock?'

Novar nodded as he turned to face the monolith. 'We pray to the Rock God for water, but he is displeased.' He waved to a female to join them. Anne noticed that her eyes were wet with tears. 'We have left a sacrifice for him, but it has not been enough to appease him.'

Jason looked suddenly concerned. 'Sacrifice?'

'Let the Unknowns through!' the priest shouted and a path was made for them through the crowd. Anne and Jason took their places on a low rock that served as a seat. As they sat down, the strange creatures shuffled forward to pinch at their skin and feel their clothing.

'They are hairless creatures,' declared an older female. 'They need these soft layers to keep them warm.'

'They're called clothes,' Anne smiled, and the word was repeated back to her.

'Tell us about your Rock God,' Jason said, keen to get to the heart of the matter.

Novar drew himself up to his full height and stamped his staff on the ground.

'We pray to the Rock God for water. If we are pure, He provides it in abundance. But recently, He has spurned our requests.'

'There's water outside,' Jason interjected. 'Plenty for all of you.' His words were met with audible gasps from those around him.

'Outside is death,' the priest intoned. 'Fire burns in the lungs of those who travel there.'

'The acidic air,' nodded Anne. 'They've never been outside.'

Jason was wide-eyed. 'So you've never seen daylight?'

The creatures shrugged and repeated the word. 'What is daylight?' Novar asked.

Jason pointed up to the beam of light shining on the rock. 'That is daylight, shining from the outside.'

There was another gasp.

'That is the Rock God's all-seeing eye!' The priest bellowed. 'It watches over us all, keeping us safe.'

'I see.' Jason said, deep in thought. 'But what was that about a sacrifice?'

The sobbing woman stepped forward. 'We have been without water for so long,' she began. 'The mosses on which we feed have grown dry. The fungi have failed. We have prayed to the Rock but still He sends us none. He is displeased.'

Anne leaned forward. 'How do you know?' she asked, gently.

'When He is pleased,' interrupted the priest, 'He cries tears of happiness and water falls from his eye.'

'You mean water falls down the shaft of light?' asked Jason, straining his neck to look up.

'The source must be blocked somewhere,' Anne muttered to her friend.

'My husband believed in the power of Nature,' the primitive woman continued. 'He was convinced he could make the water flow again without praying to a god.' She dabbed at her tears with a hairy hand. 'He was the bravest of us all,' she sobbed. 'He gave his life that we should have water.'

Anne was listening intently. 'What did he do?'

The woman steeled herself to tell the story. 'He made his way to a place we know as The Balanced Rocks. The boulders there have stood on the edge of falling for generations. It was his plan to loosen them so that they might fall.' She sobbed again. 'He never returned.'

'He is with our god now,' said the priest, solemnly.

The woman rounded on him, suddenly, her wide eyes burning with defiance. 'Then where is the water?' she asked.

There was an ominous silence in the cavern. The beams of light glancing off the rock cast strange shadows on the wall.

'We have been praying for an answer,' Novar said at last.

'Perhaps *they* are the answer!' came a voice. 'The Unknowns have come to us just in time.'

Anne looked at Jason, a worried look on her face.

A look of realisation dawned on Novar's face. 'Of course!' he bellowed. 'One sacrifice was not enough!'

'What?' Jason looked to Anne as the penny dropped.

'Our god is in need of further appeasement.' Nova had his arms outstretched as if conjuring spirits to appear before them. 'The two Unknowns will appease him and there will be water!'

'No!' screamed Anne. 'Our deaths will not bring you water!'

Just as the crowd pressed down upon them, the light shaft from the roof suddenly faded. The effect in the cavern was immediate. Without the reflected beams from the shining rock, it succumbed to an eerie darkness.

'The dark hours have begun,' intoned the priest. 'Lock up the Unknowns until the light hours return.'

Jason breathed a sigh of relief. If nothing else, they had just been granted a little time. Several of the primitives stepped forward and grabbed them by the arms, pulling Anne and Jason to a deep pit in the ground.

Their landing was soft but awkward. A layer of moss cushioned their fall, but Jason caught his shoulder on the wall as he fell. He gave a help of pain as he tried to right himself on the pit floor. Anne looked up to see the silhouettes of retreating heads. They were alone. She reached for her wrist mounted computer pad.

'Zeet?' she whispered. 'Did you get all that?' She quickly adjusted the device's volume so that the robot's reply wouldn't be too loud.

'Affirmative,' came the muted response. 'Are you both alright?' There was concern in his voice.

'We're fine,' Jason hissed, rubbing his shoulder. 'No thanks to our friends out there.'

Anne shot him a sympathetic look. 'Who would have thought an observation mission could be so exciting?'

Jason smiled ruefully. 'So what do we do now?'

'Zeet?' Anne whispered. 'I want you to scan the cave system and look for evidence of a recent rock fall. Relay it to my computer pad.'

'The Balanced Rocks?' Jason asked.

Anne nodded. 'We can't be sure that man died. What if he's injured and trapped?' She saw Jason's eyes light up. 'Looks like your mundane science mission just became a rescue,' she beamed.

Jason rose to his feet and dusted himself down, the pain in his shoulder all but forgotten. Anne pulled her hand from the backpack to reveal half a dozen pitons and a small hammer. Tearing at Jason's shirt where he had snagged it on his fall, she ripped a square of material loose and wrapped it round the hammer head. Placing each piton in turn against the rock face, she tapped gently until each had gained purchase. A soft beep from her computer pad alerted her to a message.

'Zeta's sent through a map with a likely site marked,' she said, quietly, showing Jason the screen. 'Looks like it's a hundred metres behind us.' With a nod to Jason, she began to scale the wall to the top of the pit. Peering over the lip, she saw the cave was now deserted. 'They've gone,' she whispered behind her and Jason hoisted himself up onto the first piton. As she scrambled over the edge, Anne used the screen on her computer pad to light the way. She scurried to a corner in the rock and waited for her companion to join her.

'Good idea,' said Jason as he scurried towards her. He tapped her computer pad. 'Not as bright as the torches.'

'The Balanced Rocks are that way,' she indicated a cleft in the cavern wall just ahead of them.

'Just a moment.' Jason laid a hand on her arm. 'Say this guy survived and we bring him back, won't that prove Novar's point for him? He'll claim the water isn't flowing because there was no sacrifice.'

'We have to reason with him, Jason. If we can get that water flowing, perhaps he'll see the light.' She smiled at her own weak joke then gestured that he follow her across to the small opening in the rock.

Squeezing through, Anne led the way, following directions from the map on her computer pad. Once again, they were forced to crouch low in some parts, then climb up or down almost vertically in others. At last they reached the site of The Balanced Rocks.

Now at a safe distance from the main cavern, Anne and Jason switched on their torches to illuminate the scene. Jason let the air whistle between his teeth. Ahead of them, a precarious formation of rocks teetered dangerously on the edge of toppling.

'Look there!' Anne indicated to an area of recent displacement. There seemed to be a gap in the formation's structure, beneath which was a pile of shattered rocks. 'Do you suppose that's where he fell?'

Jason scrambled over the debris, probing the shadows with his fingers.

'Wait!' called Anne, suddenly. Jason stopped in his tracks. He could hear it, too. A faint, rasping voice calling for help.

'It's coming from over here,' he called back, and Anne climbed the rock to join him. Between them, they lifted some of the smaller rocks away to reveal a hairy leg.

'It's got to be him!' Jason cried as he clawed at the debris with his hands. Clearing away the larger rocks, he revealed an arm, a shoulder and finally a face, smudged and smeared with dust.

'He's alive!' Anne exclaimed. She reached forward to cradle the man's head as Jason cleared the remaining rocks from his body.

'Help me,' the man rasped.

'You're going to be fine,' Anne soothed, trying to keep her voice calm. She punched a button on her computer pad. 'Zeet? We need help. Send Alpha with medical supplies.'

'He's on his way,' came Zeta's reply.

Anne thought for a moment. 'And look into the local topography. Try and see what might be blocking the water supply to these caves.'

'Will do,' chirped Zeta and the comms clicked off.

Just as Anne leaned forward to calm her patient, she saw his big eyes grow even wider. He had evidently seen something behind her. Spinning round, she was just in time to see a fresh rock fall bearing down on them. The boulders found their mark, crashing into the little party and pinning them to the ground. A blow to the head left Anne slipping into unconsciousness, but not before she saw Novar and his distinctive grey hair retreating from the scene of the accident.

With the morning came the return of the shaft of light from the cavern roof. The tribe had gathered again, but this time they held firebrands in their hands. Anger at their prisoners' escape had turned to triumph at their capture.

Novar had woken his fellow tribespeople in the night to lead them to The Balanced Rocks. There they had found the Unknowns lying unconscious among the rubble. Next to them they had found Jaxim, the man who had taken it upon himself to free the Rock God's tears.

Now, all three of them were tied to the glistening monolith at the centre of the cave. They were still unconscious, slumped forward against the straps that tied them to the rock. Beneath them, a pile of dried moss and roots had been placed at their feet. The High Priest of the Rock stood next to them, his staff ablaze and his manner agitated.

'You can see how our god deals with His enemies,' he proclaimed to his congregation. 'He smote them with rocks so they might sleep until their hour of reckoning.' He held his staff high for effect. 'That hour is come!'

A great cheer rose from the assembled throng, loud enough to wake the three prisoners. As Anne tried her best to focus, Jason strained against the straps that held them. No use, he thought. They were held fast. Anne let out a scream.

'Who are these people?' demanded Jaxim. 'What are you doing to us?'

'These are the Unknowns, your partners in your efforts to deny the power of the Rock God.'

'I have never seen them before in my life!' Jaxim insisted.

Novar leaned in close, his face distorted by the flickering flames. 'And yet you were found together at The Balanced Rocks.'

'We were trying to help him,' Jason hissed. 'It's what we do.'

'You would deny our god!' Novar screamed. 'It was His will that this man should die and so bring the water we need!'

'But he didn't die,' Anne said, desperately trying to reason with him. 'If it was your god's will that he should die, then why is he still alive?'

Novar spread his arms wide to address the crowd. 'See how they question our god?' He was greeted by murmurs of agreement, but Jason could see some of the tribe was unsure. 'He moves in mysterious ways,' he continued. 'He saved one man's life so that He might have three!'

The crowd cheered again, but more muted this time. A few of the primitives raised their burning torches whilst others looked around them, suddenly uncomfortable.

'Perhaps it is His will that they should all live.' The lone voice caused a hush in the cave. Several of the creatures turned to see who it belonged to. Jaxim's wife stood against a far wall, observing proceedings. Tellingly, she held no firebrand. 'How are we to know what the Rock God wants?' There were gasps from the crowd. Several of the primitives looked to Novar for his reaction. He stood, inscrutable, his grey hair glistening in the light from the fire. 'It seems that everything that happens is ascribed to Him. If the water comes, it is His will. If it does not, it is His will.' The tribespeople looked nervously around them. One or two of the braver creatures nodded in agreement and looked to their high priest for explanation.

'I am the High Priest of the Rock!' Novar bellowed. 'Our god speaks through me!'

'But how do we know you speak truth?' The woman asked, boldly.

Sensing the crowd turning against him, Novar looked suddenly desperate. 'Those who question my position will be burned with the Unknowns! The Rock God will be appeased and send more water!'

'But, if He does not?' Another voice rang out. 'Will that be His will also?'

'Perhaps it is His will that we should die of thirst,' called another.

'Or that the Unknowns should help us!'

Novar was furious. 'Blasphemy!' he cried. 'We must appease our god!'

'We *can* help you,' Anne shouted above the din. There was an immediate silence.

'You are blasphemers!' Novar screamed.

'Listen to her,' came another voice. 'If they can help us, we should let them.'

Jason leaned as close as he could to his companion. 'You sure about this Anne?'

Anne nodded and whispered back. 'Trust me,' she said.

Jason shot her a questioning look. 'Always,' he whispered back, resigned.

'How can you help?' The woman stood forward, her wide eyes fixed on Anne.

'If I can make the water flow,' Anne pleaded, 'Will you let us go?'

'We will let you go!' There was a cacophony of agreement among the crowd.

'And there will be no sacrifice?' Anne asked.

'We will let you go,' the woman promised.

Anne looked around at the hopeful faces and felt a responsibility to free them from their superstition. She bent her head as far as she could towards her computer pad. 'Ready, Zeta?'

'She consorts with false gods!' screamed Nova. 'The

Unknowns are not to be trusted. They will bring destruction upon us all!' Before anyone could stop him, he sprang forward and lowered his flaming torch. The moment it came in contact with the flame, the litter of dried moss and roots combusted.

Jason shifted where he stood to try and avoid the flames licking at his ankles. 'Any time now would be good, Zeet!' he called into Anne's computer pad. Behind him, Jaxim had his eyes squeezed shut. He was mumbling something beneath his breath as he fought to keep calm. Jason realised he was praying.

'His prayers will not save him now!' Novar screamed. 'He has forsaken his god and will be punished by the flame!'

The crowd, unsure how to react to the strange events unfolding before them, looked from Novar to the fire, then to the three prisoners tied to the rock. In need of comfort, they joined Jaxim in his prayer. Soon, the cavern was echoing to the sound of holy ritual.

Anne could feel the flames growing higher around her. Sweat was beginning to prick her forehead and sting her eyes. She looked to Jason for encouragement. 'Zeet won't let us down,' he said. He had never looked so certain of anything.

And then, just as Anne was beginning to lose hope, the water came. It was a slow trickle at first, then a stronger stream.

'Look!' called a voice from the crowd. 'Water!'

Faces were raised to the hole in the rock. 'You see!' Novar boomed in triumph. 'The Rock God is appeased! He is sending water!'

'No,' said the woman, pointing to the fire around the rock. 'The water is quenching the flames. He does not need their sacrifice.'

The crowd followed her gaze to see the flames dissipating. 'Let them go!' The cry was taken up by the congregation and soon the cavern rang with demands for the prisoners' release. Three of the more burly primitives pushed their way forward to untie them. Jaxim ran to embrace his wife as the crowd cheered.

'How did you do it, Zeet?' Jason demanded, his face a picture of relief.

'We scanned the local area,' came the response from Anne's wrist. 'A recent surface storm had diverted a stream from its course; a stream that provided water to the underground cave system. We reconfigured our weapons systems to blast a new course for the water. It should flow for decades to come.'

Anne smiled in gratitude and snapped the comms off. She caught Novar's eye as she did so. It wouldn't do for him to overhear her consorting with false gods.

Jaxim and his wife walked forward as the crowd bowed low behind them. 'We have lacked effective leadership for years,' Jaxim began. 'For too long, we have been in thrall to superstition. It is time for us to change. It would be an honour if you would stay and lead us into the light.'

The crowd behind him took up the cry. 'Lead us! Lead us!' Novar looked more uncertain than ever of his position.

Anne and Jason shared a look. 'That's very kind,' Anne said with a smile, 'but we have work to do.'

'What work?' Jaxim asked.

Jason looked at the torrent of water falling behind him in a steady stream. 'Like I said,' he beamed, 'we help people.'

'Luckily, they are a benevolent people, and the High Priest was forgiven.' Anne completed her report to the Science Chief as Jason sat beside her on the flight deck.

'Most interesting,' nodded the Science Chief from the screen. 'In many ways, they mirror early religious cultures here on Earth. I shall be fascinated to see the full findings of your mission.'

'I'm sending them to you now,' said Anne as she reached out to a button on the console. 'I'm sure you'll agree they make for interesting reading.'

The chief smiled. 'Well done, IGR4. You have done well. You and Jason are a credit to The League of Planets.'

'Thank you, sir,' said Jason as he leaned back lazily on his chair. 'But could I make a request?'

The chief nodded. 'Name it.'

'No more observation missions, please,' said the young pilot with a smile. 'They're far too exciting.'

THE STOWAWAY

Jason and Anne were feeling distinctly uncomfortable. With their two robots beside them, they stood in a vast hall faced with the massed ranks of the Mantosian military. A band played stirring, marshal music. As the anthem came to an end, the assembled soldiers gave their smartest salute. Feeling at a loss as to how to respond, Anne and Jason nodded back. Cameras at the back of the auditorium caught their every expression and beamed the pictures across the entire planet, as well as to two giant screens hung at either side of the hall. Anne shuddered as she saw her own face looming over the scene.

'Comrades,' came a disembodied voice, 'please remain standing for District Leader Kran.'

An enormous thundering sound filled the hall. Anne felt her heart race until she realised it was simply the sound of many thousands of hands coming together in resounding applause. A rather small man took to the stage with them, although he looked huge on the screens. He was dressed in a simple black suit and red tie, his blonde hair slicked back across his head.

He basked in the applause for a moment or two, then beckoned the crowd to be silent. Jason noticed that they seemed reluctant to stop, or at least to be *seen* to stop. He couldn't help but flick his eyes to the exits where soldiers in full combat gear stood guard, their weapons raised and ready.

'Comrades,' began Kran as the applause finally died away, 'here we have, standing before us, a perfect example to us all. An example of duty without regard to one's own safety. An example of how the greater good must prevail over the individual and how the individual is nothing but a vessel for the state.'

The two pilots shuffled uneasily where they stood, feeling even more uncomfortable. Anne had the distinct feeling they were being used.

Looking out into the crowd, Jason saw a young woman being manhandled to the exit. She had clearly not been fulsome enough in her applause for the District Leader. Jason caught Anne's eye and shot her a worried look. 'The sooner we're out of here, the better,' he whispered. Anne nodded in agreement.

Kran was continuing on his podium, leaning closer to the cluster of microphones placed in front of him.

'When our glorious bridge was sabotaged by Vorian terrorists, we were forced to issue a distress call.' He turned to the two pilots and their robots. 'And these faithful servants to the state rallied to our cause!'

There was another thunderous round of applause. Jason fought against the instinct to wave, while Anne let her gaze fall to the floor.

Kran smiled obsequiously at the two friends then turned his attention to the screen. 'Let's see their heroic efforts in the cause of Mantos.'

The lights dimmed in the hall and the assembled crowd turned as one to the giant screens, all under the watchful eyes of the armed guards.

Video footage of a damaged bridge played before them. It spanned the two sides of a valley, carrying a monorail across four wide arches. The two central stanchions had collapsed, leaving the severed rail dangling precariously in the air. The drop was over 300 metres to a small settlement on the valley floor.

As the camera, seemingly mounted in a flying drone, zoomed away from the bridge to follow the monorail into the open countryside, the picture settled on an automated train, thundering out of control along the track. The universal sign for 'Radioactive Material' was daubed on its many carriages. It was only a matter of time before it reached the bridge and tumbled to its destruction, destroying the town beneath and condemning the entire country to a nuclear disaster.

The crowd in the hall gasped in awe as Intergalactic Rescue 4 suddenly hove into view. With thrusters firing, it hovered above the train. Jason remembered the moment well, but even he couldn't help but be excited by the footage.

IGR4 turned to survey the scene. Just moments away, the train rumbled on its inexorable course. With a hiss of hydraulics, grappling hooks were released from the underside of the rescue craft. The hooks dropped down to the dangling monorail and with a hum of electricity, magnetised to the metal. The lines grew taut as their winches were engaged. IGR4 strained against the unforgiving metal rail as, slowly, it began to bend. Just as the train sped into view, the rescue ship gave a final burst of power and lifted the rail into place. IGR4 took the strain as the train thundered across the bridge. It lurched to one side as it ran onto the severed rail, but the ship above kept it steady. Only once the train was safely on the other side, did it let it go. The fatigued metal buckled and snapped from the rest of the rail and fell to the valley floor, narrowly missing a street of dwellings. Now, IGR4 gave chase. It wasn't enough that it had prevented the train from falling to its destruction. Now, it had to be stopped.

The drone camera rose and fell as it followed the ship along the line to the careering train. A hatch opened on its hull and a small, box-like robot was lowered to the train roof. It was Zeta. The camera zoomed in as the droid cut a hole in the cab's ceiling and disappeared inside. Within minutes there was a screeching of wheels and a shower of sparks on the line. The train drew to a halt and the little robot was winched to safety.

The lights snapped back on in the hall and, once again, there was rapturous applause.

'Comrades,' began Kran as the clapping stopped, 'it is my honour to present the crew of Intergalactic Rescue 4 with their medals. They each, from this time forward, are to be known as Heroes of the Republic.'

In turn, the crew of IGR4 stepped forward to have their medals hung round their necks. Even Alpha and Zeta were awarded magnetic medallions. As they stepped back in line, the District Leader led the crowd and band in a spirited rendition of the Mantosian National Anthem. Once again, Jason thought, there was an unspoken competition to see just who could seem the most patriotic.

'Well, that was weird.' Jason shook his head in disbelief as he sat in the canteen aboard IGR4. Mantosian food was dull and uninspiring so he was looking forward to the pancakes and syrup in front of him. He felt the ship lifting into orbit as he tucked in.

'Certainly was,' agreed Anne as she sipped from her cup of coffee. 'But I'm still glad we could help.' Inside, she was feeling a sense of dread. On their return to the ship, she had checked the coordinates of the rescue with Alpha. Sure enough, just as she had feared, the planet lay exactly in the range of the anomalous transmissions. For some reason, Jason was intent on taking Intergalactic Rescue 4 to a specific area of space whilst covering his tracks. She took another sip of her coffee. Somehow, she didn't think now was the best time to confront him.

'Now, I've just got to work out where to hang my medal.' Jason swung back on his chair, licking syrup from his lips. 'I suppose I could put it on the shelf with my Perfect Pilot award from the Academy.' He winked. 'Perfect score, three times in a row.' It wasn't the first time Jason had mentioned it in the months he had known Anne, so perhaps he shouldn't have been surprised by her not being particularly impressed. He was surprised however, that Anne had dropped her coffee to the floor and was staring over his shoulder at the door behind him. Swivelling on his chair to follow her gaze, Jason's jaw hung open in shock. There, in the doorway, stood a young woman, her eyes full of fear.

'What the— ' Jason jumped instinctively from his chair.

'Please,' the woman began, trembling. 'I mean you no harm.'

Anne pressed a button on a comms panel on the table. 'Zeet! Alpha!'

'Can I be of assistance, Ms Warran?' came Alpha's voice.

'Alpha, we have an intruder on board.'

The response was immediate. A loud klaxon blared throughout the ship. The lights flashed red in warning.

'Scanning for intruder,' Alpha beeped from the comms panel.

'It's okay, Alpha,' called Jason wearily above the noise, 'she's here in the canteen.' He looked to where the woman stood, her hands over her ears. 'I don't think she means any harm.'

'The intruder may be armed,' Alpha warned.

Jason shook his head. 'If she was armed, I think we'd

know by now.' He was losing patience with the alarm. 'Can you knock that noise off? We'll let you know if we need you.'

The klaxon was silent.

'Also,' said Anne, wryly, 'remind me to talk to you about our security protocols.' She switched off the comms with a sigh.

'Wait.' Jason had a confused look on his face as he looked the stranger up and down. 'I know you.'

'What?' Anne was suddenly by his side, perplexed. 'How?'

Jason was thinking hard. 'I saw you in the hall in Mantos.' The woman looked more sheepish. 'You were being removed by the guards.'

Anne could tell the woman was no threat. She was dressed in the utilitarian garb of a Mantosian prisoner, a world away from the smart uniform Jason last saw her in.

'How did you get on board IGR4?' Anne asked.

'I escaped.'

'From the guards?' Anne was amazed.

The woman nodded. 'I was detained in a holding room at the hall. They were planning to take me to a maximum security prison just as soon as they could.'

'Why?' Jason's eyes were wide. 'What did you do?'

The woman's eyes filled with tears. 'I fell in love,' she said, simply.

Suddenly, the ship shook. Anne grabbed at the wall to steady herself as Jason's breakfast fell from the table to the floor.

The comms bleeped from the table. 'We have company,' Zeta reported. 'A Mantosian pursuit ship. It's District Leader Kran, and he's none too pleased with us.'

Anne looked to her co-pilot. 'Let's get to the flight deck,' she said.

District Leader Kran did not look as happy as when Anne last saw him.

'District Leader,' snapped Jason as he strapped himself into his pilot's seat, 'can you explain why your pursuit ship is firing on us?'

'You have something of ours,' Kran glowered from the screen. He was on the starkly furnished bridge of his ship.

'You realise,' began Anne, sharply, 'that firing on a League of Planets ship without due cause is in violation of more treaties than I've got time to list?'

Kran looked stern. 'You have facilitated the escape of Doctor Shervan, one of our lead scientists. You have taken her without the permission of the Workers' Party of Mantos and the General Democratic Committee of the Republic.'

'She's not your property, District Leader Kran,' Anne fumed.

'She is a worker of the State of Mantos,' Kran shot back. 'We demand her return at once.'

'I think we'll consult her first,' Anne snapped. She looked around to see a fearful Doctor Shervan had made her way onto the flight deck. She hovered by the door, determined to keep out of Kran's sight. Anne gave her a reassuring smile.

'Doctor Shervan owes a debt to the society that has fed her, clothed her and given her an occupation,' Kran asserted.

'Perhaps you should consider what she has given you in return?' said Anne, brazenly. 'I'm sure she has been a faithful servant.'

Kran leaned forward to stab his finger at the screen. 'If you leave with that woman, you will be in direct contravention of our laws. You have one hour to comply. If you engage your engines, you will be destroyed along with your ship.' With that, he snapped his screen off.

Anne and Jason sat in silence for a while, then turned to face their guest.

'Let's go grab a coffee,' said Jason at last, and he led both Anne and the stowaway back to the canteen.

Shervan cradled her cup in her hand as she spoke. 'I worked on a joint scientific project with the Vorians.' She blew on her hot coffee to cool it. 'Every now and then relations between our two countries are warm enough to allow cooperation, but it is only ever temporary. Something always happens to wreck the peace. In this case, the attack on the bridge which the District Leader blames on Vorian terrorists.'

'Does he have proof?' Jason asked.

'There is never any proof. There are even some who believe the Mantosian Special Guard is responsible, although no one would say so publicly.'

'Why would they do that?' asked Anne, pulling her chair closer to the table.

'Voria is a free country,' Shervan explained. 'Their government is open and democratic so Kran considers it a threat. If relations get too close, he fears the Mantosians will see what they are denied.'

Anne nodded. It was the same with authoritarian regimes across the galaxy. The biggest fear being their people getting a taste for freedom. As Anne looked round, she saw Alpha meandering along the corridor outside, no doubt busying himself with some maintenance.

'What project were you working on?' Jason asked, enthralled.

'An infinite, efficient power source with no environmental cost.'

Jason whistled between his teeth. 'The Holy Grail.'

'And it was there that I met my husband.' Shervan took a sip of her coffee.

'Husband?' Anne was eager to hear more.

Shervan nodded, her eyes moist with tears. 'His name is Edric. We fell in love quickly and married while we could.' She wiped the tears from her eyes and met Anne's gaze. 'And now I want to rejoin him in Voria.'

'So the Mantosian authorities heard of your marriage?' Jason was thinking through the day's events. 'Is that why they arrested you at the ceremony today?'

Shervan nodded. 'It is forbidden for a Mantosian to marry outside their culture. I was threatened with a life of hard labour in the salt mines.' She shook her head. 'I had to escape.'

Anne reached out a hand. 'And we were your opportunity.'

'I managed to get away from the guards while they were distracted.' Shervan sniffed. 'I ran and ran until I found myself in the docking bay. And there was your ship. My way out.'

With Shervan resting in the guest quarters, Anne and Jason convened on the flight deck.

'What do we do?' Jason looked defeated.

'This is too big an issue for us to deal with,' Anne said, sadly. She reached for the comms panel. 'I'm calling Earth Control.'

The screen was filled with static before the connection was made. Millions of light years were traversed in microseconds as carefully positioned relay stations carried the signal back to Earth. Finally, a smartly dressed woman appeared before them.

'Anne,' she smiled, 'Jason. I hope you two have been keeping out of trouble?'

Jason sat back in his seat while Anne explained the situation. It struck him that this was the most complicated mission he had yet been involved with. Rescues he could cope with. Death defying feats he excelled at. But, politics? Jason scratched his head. Some things were best left to others.

'I'm sorry, Anne,' the woman was saying from the screen, 'but I'm afraid you have to return her to her people. You must not interfere with the internal affairs of other societies. That is not your job.'

Anne nodded sadly as she reached to switch the comms off. 'Well,' she said to Jason, 'looks like we got our answer.'

Just as she swung off her seat, she saw Alpha had entered the flight deck on his maintenance round. As she watched the little droid plug himself into the ship's systems, Anne couldn't shake the feeling that he had been listening to every word.

'I'm sorry,' said Jason. 'I wish there was more we could have done.'

'I understand,' Shervan replied.

Having allowed Kran's pursuit ship to draw level, the little party stood by IGR4's airlock door to say their goodbyes.

Anne reached out to squeeze the woman's arm. 'Perhaps there will be another way.'

Shervan smiled, kindly. 'I don't think so,' she said. 'but thank you for your friendship. I'm sorry for getting you into so much trouble.'

'Forget about it,' said Jason as he released the lock. The door swung open. Shervan looked down the docking arm to the Mantosian ship. Its hatch stood open in readiness to receive her. Through the door, Anne could see two armed guards, their guns raised.

'They don't look too pleased to see me,' Shervan laughed, dryly, and she stepped through the airlock door. It swung shut behind her, and Anne and Jason looked through the window as she made her way to the other craft. They watched, helpless, as she was grabbed by one of the guards and pulled inside. The hatch was slammed shut and the docking arm released. In moments, the pursuit craft had disappeared and Doctor Shervan with it. Anne let go a sigh. Looking around her, she saw Jason and Zeta walking back to the flight deck. But there was no sign of Alpha.

'Thank you.' District Leader Kran looked supremely satisfied at the command console of his ship. 'I am glad you saw sense at last.'

'We were complying with The League of Planet's directives, that is all.' Anne refrained from pointing out that, had she been in charge, things might well have turned out differently.

'You will always be welcome in Mantos,' the District Leader smiled. 'So long as you respect our culture.'

'We will,' Jason interjected. 'But we reserve the right to question it.'

Just as Kran was about to reply, an alarm sounded from his command console. He looked down to the readout. 'What is the meaning of this?'

Anne looked suddenly worried. 'What's happened?'

'My engines have stalled.' Kran looked furious. 'I can only imagine this is a ruse to prevent me from taking Doctor Shervan.' He pressed at the buttons on his console.

'What are you doing?' asked Jason.

'Sending a communique to The League of Planets expressing my deepest concern,' Kran thundered. 'I expect an immediate explanation, and I expect those involved to be punished.' The District Leader glared accusingly from the screen.

'You can't think that *we're* responsible,' Jason pleaded. He saw that Anne was deep in thought. 'We returned the doctor as requested.'

As the District Leader continued to rant at her co-pilot, Anne saw her opportunity to slip from her chair unnoticed.

Walking softly from the flight deck, she made her way through the corridors and walkways to find Zeta in the computer control room.

'Zeet? You got a moment?'

Zeta swivelled from his task and disconnected a mechanical arm from the console behind him. 'Of course,' he bleeped.

Anne squatted down to look directly into his visual sensors. 'Where's Alpha?' she asked.

Zeta's systems clicked and whirred. 'Searching,' he said. Anne gnawed on her lip as she waited. Finally, Zeta completed his task. 'Alpha is not on board,' he said, simply.

'What?' Anne's eyes widened in disbelief.

'Alpha is not on board Intergalactic Rescue 4,' he repeated.

'Then where is he?'

'Searching.' Zeta clicked and whirred again. 'He is at spatial coordinates four three zero by two zero seven.'

Anne stood and moved suddenly for the door. 'Patch into his visual circuits,' she called over her shoulder as she ran, 'and beam it to the flight deck. I want to see what he's seeing.'

'What's going on?' Jason looked distressed. His conversation with District Leader Kran was not going well.

'I think I might have something.' Anne's fingers danced over the flight deck controls.

'I hold you solely responsible for the crippling of my ship,' Kran shouted from the screen. 'You can rest assured I will report this gross interference in our internal affairs to your League of Planets, and your careers will be on the line.'

Suddenly a monitor flickered into life. It showed a mesh of wires and cables and a mechanical hand blocking a vent on a long metal tube.

Jason leaned closer. 'That looks like a directional jet tube. Where is this?'

Anne pointed out the cockpit window to where the stricken pursuit ship was hanging, immobile, in space. 'There.'

'But,' Jason spluttered, 'that looks like Alpha's hand.'

'It is,' breathed Anne, her heart racing. 'He's sabotaged the ship.'

'How?'

Anne punched at the computer controls and a recording played on the monitor. It was taken from outside IGR4, the camera showing the moments when the craft was attached to the Mantosian pursuit ship.

'Look!' Jason yelled, leaping towards the screen in his excitement. At about the same time as Doctor Shervan was transferring across the docking arm, Alpha was using his inbuilt thrusters to navigate his way through space. Once at the pursuit ship, he squeezed through an inspection panel at the craft's rear and disappeared.

'*That's* where he is?' Jason's jaw hung slack. He thumped at a comms button. 'Alpha, what the hell are you doing?'

'Solving a problem, Master Stone,' the little robot replied over the speaker.

Anne was incredulous. 'What problem?'

'Doctor Shervan,' came the reply.

'Zeet,' called Jason as the little robot entered the flight deck behind Anne. 'Did you know anything about this?'

'Negative,' replied Zeta, sounding almost hurt. 'If I had, I would certainly have tried to talk him out of it.' He clicked, sternly. 'Or switched him off.'

'Alpha,' scolded Anne, 'you're putting lives in danger.'

'Negative, Ms Warran,' Alpha responded, patiently. 'If I were to unblock this vent, the engines would reignite.'

'Then what's stopping you?' Jason asked, exasperated.

'District Leader Kran.'

Anne looked as bemused as Jason felt. 'How is District Leader Kran preventing you from letting that ship go?' She glanced up at the screen to see the District Leader fuming with rage.

'By denying Doctor Shervan her human freedom of association,' Alpha replied. 'If he agrees to let her land in Vorian territory, I will unblock the vent.'

'We have orders from Earth Control to return Doctor Shervan to Mantos,' Anne explained carefully.

Alpha bleeped from the speaker. 'Not every order must be obeyed without question.'

Jason's eyebrows were raised in surprise. 'Is Alpha developing a conscience?'

Zeta whirred and clicked in alarm. 'I can only apologise,' he said.

'This is an outrage!' boomed Kran. 'Your robot is deliberately disobeying a direct order from your superiors!'

'If I may, Master Stone?' interrupted Zeta. 'I wish to talk with Alpha.'

Jason threw up his hands in exasperation. 'Oh, be my guest.'

Zeta trundled closer to the comms panel. He almost seemed to clear his throat before speaking. 'Alpha,' he began, 'you have to let that ship go. Master Stone and Ms Warran's careers aboard IGR4 are worth more to the greater good than your conscience. More, even, than the happiness of one woman.'

Alpha beeped in thought. Anne leaned into the monitor to see him slowly unblocking the directional jet tube.

'You're free to go, District Leader Kran,' Anne reported. 'Please accept our deepest apologies.'

There was something odd in Kran's look as he replied. 'In a show of good faith,' he said, thoughtfully, 'I will return your robot to you.' With that, the screen went blank. Through the cockpit windscreen, Jason and Anne watched as the Mantosian pursuit ship turned back.

'Thanks, Zeet,' said Anne, patting the little droid at her feet. 'You saved the day again.'

District Leader Kran stood on board Intergalactic Rescue 4. A chastened Alpha trundled past him as Kran looked Jason in the eye.

'Here is your troublesome robot,' he almost smiled. 'He has given me cause for much thought.'

'Oh?' Jason met his gaze. 'How so?'

Kran frowned. 'What sort of citizen are you if you cannot respect the society you live in?'

Jason took a breath as he thought. 'We believe that obeying *every* order is not the way to respect a society. Those laws must be tested and, if needed, amended.'

'You are wise beyond your years,' Kran replied. 'But, tell

me. Would you be willing to sacrifice your career to test a law you didn't agree with?'

Jason nodded, slowly. 'If it meant that law might be looked at again, and perhaps changed to benefit others.'

'You were willing to risk everything for a woman you had never met before.' The

District Leader was fighting hard to understand.

'Sure,' said Jason, breezily. 'Wouldn't you?'

At a loss, Kran shook his head and turned to the airlock. With a sigh, he made his way through the docking arm to the pursuit ship, and shut the hatch behind him.

Anne and Jason sat, dejected, in the recreation suite. It had been Jason's idea that they burn off steam with a quick knockabout with a basketball but, in truth, neither of them had the heart for it.

'I guess we should set a course for home,' Anne sighed. 'We've got to face the music sooner or later.'

As they gathered their thoughts and made their way to the flight deck, they were interrupted by an alarm.

'That's a distress call,' breathed Jason, picking up the pace.

As they entered the flight deck, they were met by Zeta. He had plugged himself into the ship's systems and was busy analysing the incoming data.

'It's from Kran's pursuit ship,' he bleeped. 'A life support systems failure.'

Anne looked suddenly worried. 'Is Alpha around?'

'Alpha is tending to the Pulse Drive. Routine maintenance.'

Anne breathed a sigh of relief as the screen flicked on. District Leader Kran appeared, an expression of concern on his face. 'I'm afraid I must prevail upon your kindness,' he said. 'We have a problem with our life support. I must return to your ship at once to effect repairs.'

Anne looked to Jason. Perhaps this was an opportunity to make amends. 'Of course,' she replied. 'We'll be standing by to receive you.'

Jason shrugged his shoulders as Anne turned to him, confused. 'Beats me,' he said, 'but this is turning into one hell of a day.'

Once again, the crew of IGR4 stood at the airlock, waiting to greet District Leader Kran. This time, he had Doctor Shervan with him. She smiled in greeting as the airlock door hissed shut behind them.

'Our droids are standing by to repair your ship,' Anne said, indicating Alpha and Zeta.

'That will not be necessary,' Kran said, much to her surprise. 'I have come to a decision.'

Shervan looked up, hopefully, as the District Leader continued. 'I have just enough life support to provide oxygen for one. There is enough to see me back to the planet's surface and safely to Mantos.'

'And Doctor Shervan?' asked Anne, carefully.

There was a pause while Kran thought through the consequences of his actions. 'I guess she's yours after all.'

Shervan was trying hard to hide her delight. She had been through enough already to know not to raise her hopes.

'This operation can't technically be called a rescue,' Kran explained, 'because *I* don't need rescuing. Doctor Shervan is therefore technically lost in space. At least,' he smiled, 'that is what I shall tell the General Democratic Committee of the Republic.'

Anne jumped with delight and pulled Doctor Shervan to her.

'Then I am free to go?' Shervan asked.

Kran nodded. 'Intergalactic law says that persons lost in space must be returned to the planet or society of their choice.' He shot a meaningful look at Jason. 'And I obey the law.'

With a smart snap of his heels and a final bow to Doctor Shervan, District Leader Kran pressed the button to release the airlock. The small party watched him through the window as he made his way through the docking arm.

'Do Mantosian pursuit ships often have problems with their life support systems?' Jason asked, suspicious.

Shervan thought. 'It's practically unknown,' she replied. 'It's a relatively simple system. I don't remember any having gone wrong before.'

Jason winked at Anne as the penny dropped. District Leader Kran had found a way to save all their reputations. 'Zeet,' he said, turning to the diminutive robot, 'does intergalactic law say anything about persons lost in space?'

Zeta clicked and whirred as he searched his databanks. 'Negative,' he said at last, 'at least, nothing that relates to choice of statehood as District Leader Kran suggested.'

'How odd,' said Anne as she led their guest towards the flight deck.

'How lucky!' Jason corrected her. 'Now, Doctor Shervan. Let me take a guess as to where you want us to drop you.'

Alpha worked alone in the computer control room. It was the night shift and Jason and Anne were asleep in their quarters. Zeta was on the flight deck, monitoring frequencies for distress calls, ready to wake the humans if the need arose.

The little robot attached himself to the ship's

communications circuits and began a search of recent encrypted transmission sweeps. He had to be careful not to make his presence known to the flight deck; Zeta was monitoring the very same circuits that Alpha was exploring.

At last, he isolated a transmission stream. Like the others before it, it was hidden amongst mundane systems reports. And like the others, it was directed to a particular quadrant of the galaxy. The contents of the communication were encrypted to a level beyond Alpha's authority but there was still information to be gleaned. Alpha realised at once that a pattern was embedded in the transmission. It matched the one he had found in all the previous communications. An eight-figure transponder code. Deciding against running the number through the ship's databanks, he thought it best to use his own. His brain was a closed system and the search would not be logged. The transponder code was matched to a ship registered with The League of Planets. So, Jason was attempting to communicate with a ship. But which one? And why so covertly? The search programme continued. At last, the transponder code was matched to a specific ship. If Alpha had been human, he would have gasped. The code belonged to a ship thought lost in time and space. Jason was trying to reach Intergalactic Rescue 1.

ICE MOON

'IGR1? Are you sure?' Anne could scarcely believe it. Having shut the door carefully behind her, she was crouched next to Alpha in the computer control room. She had even taken the precaution to dim the lights, although she wasn't entirely sure why. She was just terrified that Jason would find her.

'I'm afraid it's incontrovertible,' Alpha bleeped, sadly. 'The frequency exactly matches that of Intergalactic Rescue 1's transponder.'

'And what do the communications say?' Anne trembled.

'It seems there is no message, as such,' Alpha clarified. 'It's more an attempt to ascertain its location.'

Anne was thinking hard. 'Why?'

'Unknown.' Alpha clicked and whirred as he searched his databanks. 'It seems all information on IGR1 has been removed from The League of Planets' mainframe.'

'Removed?' Anne's jaw hung slack. 'No specs? Crew manifests? Mission logs?'

'Nothing,' Alpha buzzed.

Anne frowned. Far from clarifying the situation, Alpha's investigations had left her more confused than ever.

Far below the surface of the lunar ocean, an impossible thing was happening. Hoshi and Cramer were getting on just fine. Hoshi was 30 years' Cramer's junior and, usually, that was a bone of contention. Differences in approach to their work were seen as evidence of their age gap. Cramer was dogged, particular and did things by the book. By contrast, Hoshi was happy to fly by the seat of her pants, to experiment with new ideas and 'think outside the box'. That phrase annoyed Cramer intensely. She would roll her eyes whenever she heard it. 'What box?' she would ask, exasperated. 'Why do you talk such nonsense?'

'You've got to be open to new ideas,' Hoshi replied once. 'After all, it's new ideas that put us on this moon.'

Cramer sighed. 'And it's new ideas that ruined our home.'

On the seabed, they had no view of the ruined planet beneath them. But both Hoshi and Cramer knew it was in trouble. Great clouds of toxic gas swirled in the atmosphere. The rivers, seas and lakes were poisoned with noxious chemicals. The ever-expanding population was hungry. From their subaquatic base, surrounded by the awesome tranquillity of the lunar sea, it was difficult to remember quite how desperate things were on Sandreen.

'What's on the itinerary today?' Hoshi asked over breakfast one morning. The habitat was cramped but comfortable enough. Large flexiglass windows allowed for impressive views of the ocean bed. Lights had been mounted outside the structure to illuminate the site.

Cramer let her eyes wander along the beds of weeds as she thought.

'Nothing exciting,' she replied, chewing on her protein biscuit. 'We need to up the nutrient content in the squirmers' food. And then there's the perimeter boundary to look into.'

'I've been thinking about that,' said Hoshi through a mouthful of food. Cramer felt her spirits sink. If Hoshi had been thinking, there was going to be trouble. Or, at least, a confrontation. 'I was wondering if we could harvest energy from the tidal boom to power the boundary.'

Cramer rolled her eyes. 'It would blow the circuits,' she said, as calmly as she could. 'They're not built to withstand that kind of power.'

'I could fit an adapter,' Hoshi began.

'It wouldn't work,' Cramer interrupted. She put her biscuit down on her plate. 'Look, I've been farming squirmers for 15 years. If we start diverting energy from the boom, we put the whole habitat at risk.' As if to prove her point, a fluorescent strip light flashed on and off behind her. 'Things are precarious enough as it is.'

Hoshi sat back in her chair. 'Are you ever going to listen to anything I say?'

'Sure,' replied Cramer, dryly. 'Just as soon as you know as much as me.'

There was no answer to that, and Cramer knew it. Hoshi realised she couldn't win. The two women continued their meal in silence until it was time to suit up for the day's work.

The way to the airlock was lined with loose cables and ducting. Here and there, water dropped from conduits. Though still serviceable, the habitat had clearly seen better days.

'I'll take the south pens today,' Hoshi said as she struggled into her atmospheric diving suit. It was more of a one-person articulated submersible resembling a suit of armour.

Cramer nodded. That was typical, she thought. The south pens were much quicker to patrol. Hoshi was obviously hoping to be back in her quarters for a nap before lunch. Cramer had no idea why the girl needed so much sleep.

'Fine,' she said, wearily. 'Then perhaps you can make a

start on the squirmers' nutrient mix when you get back.' She enjoyed the look of disappointment on Hoshi's face.

When they had both donned their suits, they took a few moments to check each other's seals.

'Check comms?' said Cramer, tapping her helmet.

'Checking comms,' came Hoshi's response and they gave each other a thumbs up.

Finally, they made their way to the airlock. The door opened with a hiss and they stepped through to a small holding room. Closing the hatch behind them, Hoshi leaned against a button to pressurise the space, then opened the next hatch into another chamber.

Here, with the pressure at the same level as the water outside, a large central pool gave access to the ocean beyond. As easily as if they were stepping into a hot tub, the two women lowered themselves down the fixed ladders and into the swirling maelstrom.

Their weighted boots held them to the seabed, enabling them to make their way slowly from the habitat, their progress illuminated by the great arc lights around them and the torches on their helmets.

Cramer watched as Hoshi turned away towards the south pens. Perhaps she was too hard on the girl, she thought to herself. She struggled hard to remember what she had been like at that age. Strong willed, certainly, but not quite so cocksure. Perhaps Hoshi deserved to be brought down a peg or two. Cramer sighed and made her way towards the boundary generator. It projected an energy shield around the entire facility, enabling Cramer to keep the waters around the squirmer pens pristine. This meant she could measure precisely what they were eating and monitor their nutritional intake. As she approached the generator through the murky water, she could see the boundary was fluctuating wildly.

Cramer tutted to herself. She knew Hoshi's idea was a good one. Diverting excess energy from the tidal boom above them made a lot of sense, but Cramer couldn't let her companion think she was right. Cramer shook her head. She knew the whole situation was crazy. Hoshi was a good kid. Why couldn't she just accept her ideas? Falling to her knees on the seabed, she peered closer at the generator's instruments. It looked like she'd have to——

Cramer didn't have time to complete her thought. The first thing she experienced was a loud thump that seemed to come from all around her. Before she had time to turn and look for the source of the noise, she was lifted off her feet by an aquatic shockwave that carried her beyond the energy boundary and flung her unceremoniously against an ancient reef. The water bubbled and seethed around her. As it cleared, she was finally able to look back towards the habitat. What she saw took her breath away. The entire building was crumbling. A series of further explosions ripped through the structure, the sturdy supporting walls collapsing as if they were made of sand. Cramer could see fires burning behind those huge windows, until a deluge of water quenched the flames. As the explosions petered out, the internal atmosphere escaped in great bubbles up towards the surface. A slick of oil gave the water a sickly stain. Cramer could barely believe what she was seeing.

'Hoshi,' she rasped. 'Hoshi, can you hear me?' The arc lights, deprived of their power from the habitat, flickered out as she spoke. Now she was completely dependent on her head torch. There was silence for a moment, then Cramer was sure she heard scratching over her comms.

'Yes,' came Hoshi's panicked voice. 'I'm fine. I'm fine.' Cramer felt tears of relief prick her eyes. Hoshi was breathing hard. 'What the hell happened?' she gasped.

'I have no idea,' admitted Cramer. 'But there's five

kilometres of water above us and enough air in our tanks for perhaps an hour.' They might have both survived the blast, but what now?

Hoshi caught her breath. 'Let's just hope the automated distress call got away in time.'

The cosmos split apart. With a crack of energy, Intergalactic Rescue 4 appeared through the gap in space and hung, expectantly, above the ice moon. Inside, Jason and Anne unsnapped the restraints on their pilots' chairs and leaned forward for a better view.

'The second moon of the planet Sandreen,' Zeta reported. 'The planet is showing dangerous signs of climate change, pollution and overcrowding. The moon is capable of supporting marine life beneath the ice but is otherwise hostile to life on the surface.'

'Looks chilly,' grinned Jason.

'Actually,' bleeped Zeta from the floor where he had attached himself to the ship's systems, 'the surface temperature of the moon is minus 215 degrees Celsius.'

'That's only an average,' Alpha interrupted. 'At its coldest, it reaches as low as minus 263 degrees.'

'Thank you, Alpha,' Anne smiled. 'It's always good to know the details. Now, where's that signal coming from?'

In response, Zeta flashed an image of the moon up on the screen. It showed IGR4's relative position and a glowing dot at some distance beneath the icy surface.

'It's under the water?' Jason asked.

'Some 5,000 metres down,' Zeta clarified. 'The lunar ocean is covered in a crust of ice.'

'Great,' Jason scoffed. 'Just when I thought things were going to be easy. Is it thick enough for us to land on?'

'Affirmative,' bleeped Alpha.

'Are we able to communicate?' Anne asked.

'Negative,' the little robot replied. 'The distress call was automated.'

Anne sighed. 'So we don't even know how many people are in need of rescue.'

'We need to get eyes on,' said Jason urgently. 'Alpha, prep the sub while I put us down on the ice.' Alpha beeped happily as he disconnected himself and limped from the flight deck.

Anne watched through the cockpit window while Jason leaned on the controls. As they got nearer to the moon, it was possible to make out details on the icy surface. Great ridges of thick ice reared up over smooth, glittering plains.

'There,' exclaimed Jason as he pointed through the glass. 'That's where I'll put her down.'

Anne squinted to see a flat area of ice beneath an escarpment. Judging from Zeta's image on the screen, it would put them almost exactly above the source of the distress call. With a hiss of thrusters they descended at speed, only for Jason to lean back and bring IGR4 onto the ice with the softest of landings.

'The submersible is standing ready,' Alpha reported over the internal comms.

'Great work, Alpha!' Jason swung from his chair and flashed a smile to Anne. 'Shall we?'

The sub hung in the air, suspended over an open hatch in the hull. As Jason and Anne approached in their suits and helmets, a ramp extended from the submersible and the door opened to its cramped cockpit. There was barely room for the both of them but, as they wriggled into their seats, they made space. Anne was already at the controls as Jason strapped himself in. She was reaching up to flick switches, then leaning forward to grasp the joystick. The engines sparked to life with a gentle hum as the door closed behind them and the ramp retracted.

'Ok, Alpha,' Anne said over her helmet comms. 'We're ready!'

A light flashed on the dashboard and Jason felt the tiny craft beginning to drop. The winch dropped the sub slowly through the hull to the ice below. There was a jolt as the hooks were released and drawn back into the ship. A gentle nudge on the joystick saw the submersible slide clear of IGR4 and onto the icy plain. They came to rest a few metres away from the ship. Jason took the opportunity to look behind him. It was a surreal sight. Intergalactic Rescue 4 stood on the ice of an alien moon, stark against the blackness of the lunar sky.

'Er, Anne,' he said at last. 'What do we now? The distress call came from 5,000 metres down and there's a layer of ice between us.'

'Don't worry, Jason,' Anne smiled, 'I've thought of that. She reached forward to the dashboard. 'I'm rerouting the internal heating systems to the outer hull.' She flicked switches and pulled levers as she explained. 'Specifically to the lower membrane.'

Jason nodded in admiration. The little sub was coated in a chemical membrane that enabled it to slip through water at speed. It was about to be put to a very different use.

'Here we go,' said Anne as she pushed hard on the joystick. The effect was immediate. As Jason looked out the windows, he saw the ice around them begin to crack and steam. Soon, they were surrounded by a pool of bubbling water, and the little sub began to sink beneath waves. The water level rose over the windows so that, in just a few minutes, they were metres through the ice. At last they were free of it, and Anne nudged the craft's nose down. Looking up, Jason saw a great, white ceiling stretching as far as the eye could see, the tiny hole through which they had sunk receding behind them.

'Amazing,' beamed Jason.

'Keep your eyes peeled,' Anne countered. 'We may not have much time.'

The submersible dropped like a stone through the water, its forward lights illuminating the way. Every now and then, strange shapes would drift by them in the watery gloom, but whether they were animal, vegetable or mineral, Jason couldn't tell.

'There!' he exclaimed at last.

Following his gaze, Anne saw the remains of a large structure, smouldering in the depths. A dirty smudge of debris rose from the wreck of a building.

'Let's take a closer look,' she said, grimly. 'Although I don't hold out much hope of finding anyone.' Whatever had happened, she was certain no one could have survived it.

The sub skimmed the perimeter of the habitat. Every now and then, Anne would angle it so that its headlights shone into the shattered interior.

'Nothing,' said Anne, sadly. 'Perhaps we're too late after all.'

'Wait!' exclaimed Jason suddenly, leaning forward in his seat. 'Look there!'

Anne swivelled in her seat to look where he was pointing. There, just a few hundred metres away, she could see flashing lights. It was almost as if someone was trying to signal them.

'They've seen us!'

Hoshi had convinced Cramer to meet her at the south pens and hunker down by the small maintenance pod. It took them a full half hour to reach it. They had just 30 minutes worth of air left in their mobile tanks.

Now they stood at the small window, waving their torches desperately at the submersible circling the remains of their habitat. They were relieved to see it turning towards them and within minutes, it was standing on the sea bed. Jason had scrambled to the back of the submersible and into its cramped airlock. Finally, the rear hatch opened and he stepped onto the soft sand. He couldn't help looking up and around him. The water was smudged with pollutants from the still unstable habitat and, every now and then, the swirling sediment was disturbed by smaller explosions. He felt ever increasing tremors in the sludge beneath his feet as he made his way over to Cramer and Hoshi.

'This whole area is unstable,' Cramer explained as he approached. 'The blast must have weakened the sea floor.'

'What happened?' Jason gasped over his helmet comms.

Cramer shook her head. 'We don't know. It looked like a gas leak, but who can tell?'

'Are you hurt?' Jason asked.

'No,' replied Hoshi. 'Just a little bruised from when the blast threw us clear.'

'My name is Jason Stone from The League of Planets.' He gestured back to the sub. 'Anne Warran is standing by to take you to the surface where Intergalactic Rescue 4 stands ready to lift you clear of the moon.' The ground shook violently as he spoke and Jason had to fling his arms wide to steady himself. 'And it feels like we don't have long.'

Cramer looked suddenly worried. 'My work!' she gasped.

Hoshi turned to her. 'It's too late to think of that. We need to get out of here.'

'You don't understand,' Cramer replied urgently. 'There's

15 years of scientific results in that habitat. It might just provide the answers to our problems on Sandreen.'

'Jason,' came Anne's voice over comms. 'We need to get out of here.'

Jason looked back to see his co-pilot gesturing through the submersible window.

'You go.' Cramer nudged Hoshi forwards. 'I've had an idea.'

Hoshi looked aghast. 'You're not going back to the habitat? There's nothing left.'

The ground shook again, releasing clouds of debris into the water. They could feel the currents increasing around them, threatening to pull them this way and that. The little party made their way as quickly as they could towards the sub. The little airlock door swung open to receive them.

'No,' Cramer called over the comms. 'But I can make it to the bathysphere.' She pointed beyond the submersible to where a metal sphere stood at a crazy angle on the sea floor. Seemingly it too had been dislodged by the blast and had come to rest by a rocky outcrop. An ominous rumble came from below, followed by the release of hundreds of bubbles of gas from beneath the sludge.

Hoshi seemed appalled that Cramer would decline the opportunity of rescue. 'We've got a chance to get out of here alive,' she said, aghast. 'What can you do in the bathysphere?'

'It's connected to the habitat's computer core,' Cramer explained. 'If the link is intact, I can download the data to the bathysphere's computer and save it.'

'That'll be no good if you're dead,' screamed Hoshi impatiently. 'You'll still have to get to the surface and you have less than 20 minutes of air left in your tank.'

'There will be air in the sphere,' Cramer shot back.

'Perhaps just enough to get one person to the surface. The aqua jets should still be operable.'

'You're such a stubborn old woman!' Hoshi bellowed as the ground heaved beneath their feet.

'And you've never understood the importance of my work!' Cramer seemed just as irritated with her colleague. Suddenly, the water shifted around them and a huge fissure opened up in the ocean floor.

'We've got to go, Jason!' Anne called from the sub. 'It's not safe here!'

At last they were at the sub. With so much sediment released into the water, it was getting difficult to see. Jason groped to hold the airlock hatch open and stood aside to let Hoshi in first.

'Please,' he begged. 'Let us get you to the surface. We can think about your work when you're both safe.' A sudden eddy caught him off guard and he pitched forward into the airlock. He fell to the floor with his arms flailing about him. Just as he struggled to his feet, the weight of another body pinned him down. He heard the airlock close behind him, then the throwing of bolts to seal it shut. The sub lurched suddenly.

'I've got to get out of here!' came Anne's voice, and Jason felt the submersible lift off towards the icy surface. As the water drained from the airlock, he lifted his helmet from his head and looked around him. Cramer was leaning against the hatch, breathing heavily. She held her own helmet beneath her arm as she rubbed her shoulder with her other hand.

'She tripped me and pushed me into you,' she sighed. 'She's going to get herself killed.'

Jason blinked as he took in the information. They had left Hoshi behind on the seafloor.

As the sub lifted off, Hoshi found herself tumbling down

the newly opened fissure. She reached out with her hand and managed to take a hold of a tangle of seaweed. Her fall broken, she rested for a moment to catch her breath, then heaved herself over the lip of the fissure. The crack stretched into the gloom, as far as the eye could see. She could just make out the surrounding sediment falling into it like sand through an hourglass. Standing up, she managed to get clear of a drift of sand as it slipped over the edge of the abyss, sucking rocks and debris after it. Panting hard, she focussed her sight on the bathysphere in the distance.

'What the hell are you doing, Hoshi?' came Cramer's voice over the comms.

'Saving your work,' Hoshi replied. She was having to focus her energies on putting one foot in front of the other. There was so much movement in the water around her that she felt she was making no headway at all.

'We can't come back for you,' came Jason's voice. 'It's too dangerous for us to land again.'

'I'm not asking to be rescued,' Hoshi panted.

'You were always so stubborn,' said Cramer. Hoshi smiled. 'You've got all your life to live. Why didn't you let me go?'

'Because you're Cramer Kursh,' Hoshi replied. 'The famous scientist who will feed the world.' She could see the bathysphere looming before her. 'You were my hero, growing up,' she admitted. 'I never dreamed I would ever work with you.'

She could tell the professor was shocked. 'You never mentioned that,' Cramer said.

'Of course, I didn't,' Hoshi laughed. 'Because that would mean admitting to myself that I wasn't worthy of the position.'

There was silence over the comms.

'What were you doing down there?' Anne asked as she lifted the sub's nose up to the surface.

Cramer sighed. 'Trying to save the world,' she said, sadly. 'The planet Sandreen is overpopulated. Within 10 years, we simply will not have enough food for everybody.' She rubbed her forehead with a trembling hand. 'I have been working on a new source of food. Squirmers, I call them.' She gave a weak smile. 'Nothing can live in Sandreen's poisoned oceans, but here on the moon I have been able to breed a protein rich source of food, cheap and abundant.' Jason was sure he could see tears in her eyes as she continued. 'Over the past 15 years, I have developed a fish that can live happily in these harsh conditions. It's a possible answer to our problems. We breed them up here and ship them to Sandreen. Hoshi joined me recently as I came closer to completing my work. Now she's down there, trying to save it.'

Jason reached out a hand to console her.

'I never knew she thought so much of me,' Cramer sobbed as she peered out the window to the murky depths beneath.

Hoshi had reached the bathysphere. Her legs ached from the effort of walking and her lungs burned. She could feel she was getting low on air. The exertion of walking through the turbulent water had been harder work than she thought, and she had found herself taking big gulps of precious air in spite of her predicament. She tried to steady her breathing as she leaned against the bathysphere's smooth side. She could see cracks and dents in the metal.

'I'm at the bathysphere,' she reported over comms. 'It looks damaged.'

'You need to get inside, quick,' Cramer replied. 'You've got less than five minutes of air left.'

'I know,' Hoshi gasped, 'I can feel I'm running low.' Her head was swimming after her efforts. 'Just got to get inside.'

Hoshi fell to her knees and started scrabbling at the sand with her hands. The bathysphere was a bell-shaped vessel with an open bottom, used for quick ascent and descent from the depths. As long as it was upright, there was enough air inside to last a single journey to the surface. Hoshi and Cramer had used it countless times to explore the moon's icy crust, leaving the sphere to replenish its air supply while on the surface. It was normally held suspended above the seabed on a platform so that the scientists could heave themselves up and inside where they sat safely in the air pocket within. Now, it lay at an angle on the seabed so that Hoshi had to dig beneath it to gain access.

At last, she had worked her way round the underside of the bell and was able to pull herself inside. The interior was lined with a film of sand and mud, obscuring the computer panels set into the side wall. But, worse than that, it was entirely full of water.

'It's what?' On board the submersible, Cramer was aghast.

'The water got in,' came Hoshi's voice over the comms. 'The bathysphere was damaged in the blast. I noticed cracks. There's no air inside.'

Cramer looked panicked. 'Can't we go back for her?' she pleaded, turning to Anne at the sub's controls.

'It's too dangerous,' Anne replied, trying to keep calm. 'She knew that.'

'But we'll be back aboard IGR4 soon.' Jason pointed out the window towards a gap in the ice. It was where the sub had dropped at the start of their rescue attempt. 'It's far better equipped to deal with this. It's not over yet.'

Anne leaned on the joystick to increase speed and the little submersible exited the water to slide onto the icy surface of the lunar ocean. Pulling back, she slowed the craft and brought it round. There stood Intergalactic Rescue 4, its hull shining with the sheen of a million tiny ice crystals.

'The connection's still open,' Hoshi reported into her helmet comms. Her vision was beginning to blur and her hands felt heavy. Every now and then she would feel a tremor from beneath which reminded her just what a precarious position she was in. 'Great,' she muttered to herself. 'If I don't suffocate I'm going to get shaken to death.'

'Have you accessed the habitat's computer core?' came Cramer's voice.

'Yes,' Hoshi responded. She stabbed at the buttons on the console. She tried to blink away the feeling of tiredness, but her eyelids were heavy. 'I need a password.'

From somewhere, she heard Cramer's voice echoing. 'It's MAGENTA,' she said, and Hoshi heard her spelling it out. Letter by letter, she moved her index finger to punch at the keyboard. With her extremities so numb, she had to hold one hand steady with the other and move it carefully along the console. At last, a series of characters and digits scrolled down the screen.

'That's it!' she heard Cramer exclaim.

'Hoshi,' came another voice. It was young and male and she was sure she recognised it. 'Transmit that data to IGR4. You need to pair with our data hub and we'll do the rest.' His voice sounded like it was coming from a long way off. 'Look for the icon on your screen.'

Hoshi's ears were ringing. She tried to peer at the screen through the murky water. A shape resolved itself on the monitor. It was a small representation of what Hoshi assumed must be the craft above her. Falling against the console, she pressed the screen with the palm of her hand.

'We've got it!' Cramer shouted, triumphantly. 'The data's coming through! Now get yourself up here!'

Hoshi smiled, then felt her world slipping away around her. Some rational part of her brain knew she was out of air and out of time. She turned to engage the aqua jets. The controls swam before her eyes, the buttons and levers a swirl of colours and shapes. Concentrating hard, she leaned towards the ignition control and fell upon it with all her weight. Nothing. Letting go her final breath, a dreadful realisation dawned. The engines didn't work.

'Get her out of there!' Cramer screamed on the flight deck. 'She's out of air!'

'There's no time to get back down in the submersible,' Anne said, her mind racing.

Jason was thinking fast, too. 'We don't need the submersible,' he said with a grin. Throwing himself into the pilot's chair, he leaned against the controls to fire up the engines. 'Zeet!' he called. 'I want you to tell me when we're directly over the bathysphere. Anne?' He turned to his co-pilot to see her strapping herself into her chair. 'Stand by with the grappler.'

'What are you going to do!' asked Cramer as she leaned against the wall for support.

Jason swivelled round and flashed her his biggest smile. 'We're going fishing!' he boomed.

Cramer felt the ship lift into the air and turn. 'Ready the forward laser, Alpha,' Jason called. The little robot connected himself to the ship's weapons systems.

'Ready,' he chirped.

'Hold this position, Master Stone,' Zeta bleeped, suddenly. 'We are now directly above the bathysphere.'

'Firing forward laser!' Jason announced. He leaned

forward to press a button, and the sky outside the cockpit window was aflame.

Directly beneath the ship, the laser cut through the ice as if it were butter. Soon, the water beneath was boiling with the heat, the steam rising into the thin lunar atmosphere.

'Okay, Anne,' said Jason leaning back in his seat. 'Let go the grappler!'

Anne flicked the switch to release a joystick. As she grabbed at the controller, a computer monitor flickered into life. It showed a straight, perpendicular line between IGR4 and a flashing point indicating the position of the diving bell. The grappling line descended as she pulled on the joystick's trigger. Over her shoulder, Cramer watched as the line descended.

'Magnetising!' Anne announced. Jason turned back to the screen to see the grappler had reached the bathysphere and was attempting to get purchase on its smooth outer hull. 'Got it!' screamed Anne, and she pulled the joystick back as hard as she could.

Jason held the ship steady as the grappler was winched up with its load.

'Alpha!' called Anne as she pulled on the joystick. 'Prep the medlab. Zeta, take Doctor Cramer to the cargo bay and help her to carry Hoshi to a bed. 'We'll be with you just as soon as we're in orbit.'

Cramer watched as the two robots disconnected themselves and went about their business, Zeta waiting by the door for her to accompany him.

The battered bathysphere looked incongruous in the sparse, white surroundings of the cargo bay. It hung, suspended from the winch, the dregs of dirty seawater dripping from its underside. Cramer bent down to poke her head through the opening. There, she saw Hoshi sprawled on the narrow ledge that ran around the circumference of the interior. She jumped inside the bathysphere as quickly as she could, cursing her back as she felt a twinge of pain. Reaching forward, she unclipped Hoshi's helmet. She stroked her face as she whispered, feverishly.

'Hoshi? Hoshi, can you hear me?' Nothing. 'Oh, Hoshi.' Cramer began to sob. '*You* are the hero.'

Just as she had given up hope, Hoshi's eyelids flickered. 'Hoshi!' beamed Cramer. 'You made it!'

Hoshi looked around weakly. 'Doctor Cramer,' she smiled. 'I never thought I'd say this, but it's very good to see you.'

ANIMALS

With a roar of vertical thrusters, Intergalactic Rescue 4 sank below the tree line.

'It's beautiful,' exclaimed Anne as she gazed through the cockpit window. 'Like some sort of Eden.'

'It's perfect. Like Earth before we ruined it,' Jason agreed. 'Which makes me wonder why they sent a distress call.'

Beyond the trees, Anne had glimpsed a beach and rolling waves. A hazy mountain range stood a little way inland.

'Trilon is very similar to Earth in terms of size, mass and distance from its sun,' bleeped Zeta. The two robots had connected themselves to the ship's systems and were busy analysing the stream of incoming data.

'That would explain why it has taken a very similar evolutionary route,' interjected Alpha. 'You will recognise many familiar species of flora and fauna with very few differences from their Earth counterparts.'

Jason nodded. 'This place just gets better and better,' he mused. His fingers dancing over the thrust controls, he brought the ship down expertly. Switching off the engines and clicking off his restraints, he turned to Anne. 'Don't forget your swimsuit,' he grinned.

The arrival of IGR4 had attracted quite a crowd. The ship had landed in an open clearing surrounded by sturdy buildings. As

Jason made his way down the ramp, he was interested to see a mix of primitive building techniques and modern tech. The ground beneath him felt hard and metallic beneath the sand. As the locals rushed forward to greet him, he couldn't help taking a breath. They were a mixture of species. Predominantly, the population seemed to be made of apes. Jason recognised gorillas, orangutans and chimpanzees, but there were also dog and cat-like creatures, all standing at least six feet tall on their hind legs. A female wolf-like creature pushed herself forward.

'I am Laan,' she said. Jason found it difficult to read her yellow eyes.

'I'm Jason Stone,' he replied, courteously. 'This is Anne Warran and that's our ship.' He waved behind him.

'That's it?' Laan looked disappointed.

Jason laughed. He wasn't used to people being quite so underwhelmed.

'It's The League of Planets' finest,' Anne smiled to break the tension. She looked around her as she spoke. At first sight, Trilon seemed like a Paradise but, looking closer, it was as if she could see cracks in the facade. The animals looked nervous and tired. A few of them were wounded. Looking at the settlement, she saw small parties engaged in repairing some of the buildings. Beyond the clearing, she noticed a young tiger shouting instructions to a small group of deer-like creatures. They were attempting to fix a broken perimeter fence.

'You'd better tell us what's been going on here,' Anne suggested, a note of unease in her voice.

A great fire had been built in the middle of the clearing. Anne had the impression it had been built more to provide safety than warmth.

'We are the indigenous species of Trilon,' Laan was

explaining. 'It has been our home for hundreds of thousands of years. Perhaps even millions. We have worked together to make it a planet of peace.'

Jason nodded as he looked around. 'It certainly looks the perfect place to live,' he agreed.

'For a long time it was.' Laan gestured to a low table with her paws. It was festooned with fruit and wooden pitchers of juice. Anne and Jason took their food gratefully, biting into the fruit's soft flesh without having to be encouraged. 'But, recently, not so much.'

Anne finished her fruit and threw the stone into the fire. It reminded her of a peach and was probably the freshest thing she had eaten in months. 'What's the emergency?' she asked. 'We picked up a distress signal.'

'I'm sure you think we have everything,' Laan answered, enigmatically. 'The beach, the trees, our way of life.' She looked at the settlement around her with a certain pride, then turned to stare directly at Anne. 'In fact, we have only hours to live.'

Anne's jaw hung slack.

'What?' Jason could scarcely believe his ears. The settlement seemed such a peaceful place. He was sure they had their problems – the repair parties were evidence of that – but were their lives really at risk?

Laan could see the disbelief in the youngsters' eyes. 'Since the dawn of our recorded history, we have lived in peace. Trilon affords us everything for a comfortable life.' She gestured around her. 'Wood for building, water and food aplenty. With our limited technology we have built reservoirs and irrigation systems. We fish in the sea and farm on the inland plains.'

'What happened?' asked Anne, eagerly.

'Twenty years ago, the colonists came.' Laan dared her to look away. Anne swallowed hard. Jason looked at the trees and the mountains beyond in a new light. Suddenly, he sensed danger in every rustle of leaves. And he was certain they were being watched.

'At first,' Laan was continuing, 'they said they would be our friends. We traded with them, even socialised with them.' She cast her eyes to the ground as she spoke. 'But soon they showed their true colours. They began to terrorise us. They began to hunt us for our fur,' she shivered, 'and for our meat. A few of us are held captive on their farms. They want the rest of us removed from the face of the planet.'

Anne was agog. 'Who are these colonists? Where are they from?'

Laan met her gaze. 'Earth,' she said, simply. 'They are human. Like you.' She leaned forward to pour a drink from a wooden pitcher. 'At first, they were cautious.' She lapped from a cup fashioned from a coconut shell. 'We would hear them at night, skirting our perimeter fence, talking with one another. Then they got bolder.'

Anne stood with a hand on her head. She looked again at the damaged buildings. 'They broke in?'

'Initially, they were only interested in breaking our machinery or vandalising our buildings. Then they turned violent.'

Anne turned to look at her in horror. Did that explain the injured animals she had seen around the settlement?

'They come at night when we are most vulnerable.' Laan's eyes took on a haunted look. 'They break down our fences and our doors and they attack us. We have no weapons here – we've never needed them – and so we have only sticks to beat them back.' She gestured towards a passing animal, an elderly lion with a missing leg. 'Sometimes it is not enough.'

Jason cleared his throat. 'What do they want?' he asked, his voice trembling.

'They want us gone,' replied Laan, simply. 'And they want us gone by tonight.'

'Tonight? How do you know?'

Laan looked at Jason with a quizzical look. 'They told us, of course.'

Anne shook her head. She didn't know what to think. 'They *told* you?'

'They last attacked us three nights ago,' Laan explained. She stood up and beckoned the two friends to follow her to a nearby building. 'They left us this.'

Anne and Jason looked up at the building before them. On the nearest wall the words, BE GONE BY THE FULL MOON, had been daubed in capital letters.

'Concise and to the point, I suppose.' Jason puffed out his cheeks.

Laan snarled as she gestured to the wall. 'This is written in blood from a young gazelle they wounded.'

'And the full moon is…?' asked Jason, looking to the sky.

'Tonight,' Laan confirmed.

'So that's why you sent the distress call,' Anne said, turning back to look around the settlement.

'What choice did we have?' Laan sighed. 'All we have are sticks and stones. They're no match against human ferocity. They are the most dangerous species of all.'

Anne felt uncomfortable.

'We can evacuate you,' Jason said at last. 'Lift you off the planet. Take you wherever you want to go.'

Laan nodded to where Intergalactic Rescue 4 stood in the clearing. 'In that?' she scoffed.

'She's powerful,' said Jason, suddenly defensive.

'Maybe,' shrugged Laan. 'But she's not very *big*. There are over three hundred of us. Are you suggesting some of us cling on to the outside?'

Jason looked away. They couldn't get anywhere near that many people on board.

'We could take you in shifts,' suggested Anne. 'She's quick.'

Laan shook her head. 'Not quick enough. The nearest habitable planet must be light years away and you'd need to make several trips. We need to be gone by nightfall.'

Anne looked out to see the horizon was already tinged with purple. Laan led them towards the clearing and looked up at IGR4. All around them, the animals were suddenly engaged with preparations for the attack. Doors and windows were being barricaded. Pits were being dug and covered with rushes to disguise them. Large stakes were being driven into the ground, their sharpened points angled menacingly into the air.

'As far as I can see,' Laan was saying, 'there's only one way out of this.'

Anne looked at her, her eyebrows raised. 'What do you mean?'

Laan scratched her ear with a claw. 'I take it your ship is armed?'

'Of course,' answered Jason without thinking. 'Lasers, rockets, space mines.'

'Jason,' Anne was shaking her head to dissuade him from continuing. She knew where this was leading.

Suddenly understanding, Jason fought to cover his tracks. 'Of course, they're only ever intended for use in rescues.'

'*This* would be a rescue!' Laan asserted, boldly. 'Look around you. Three hundred innocent lives are at risk.'

Anne shook her head, downcast. 'We can't just use our weapons against the colonists. There has to be another way.'

'There is no other way.' Laan's jaw was set in an attitude of defiance. 'If we don't kill them, they'll kill us for sure.' Her lower lip was trembling. 'And you and The League of Planets will have our blood on your hands.'

Jason took Anne by the arm and led her away through the clearing. He was puzzled once again to feel the ground was hard and metallic beneath his feet. They stood staring through the trees to the beach beyond. As the sea rolled lazily along the shoreline, it seemed impossible that there was any threat to the animals at all.

'What are we going to do?' Anne asked.

Jason whistled through his teeth. 'Well, we can't just leave them.'

'But we can't attack the humans.'

'We could help fortify their settlement,' Jason suggested, casting about for ideas.

'Or even fight at their side.'

'With what?' asked Anne. 'Sticks and stones?' She gnawed at her lip as she thought. 'Of course, there's something we haven't considered at all.'

Jason looked at her. 'What?'

Anne looked up at the darkening sky. 'Dialogue.'

'You're going to talk to them?' Laan was exasperated.

'Why not?' Anne pleaded. 'We're human, too. Perhaps they'll listen to their own kind.'

Laan threw back her head and laughed, bitterly. 'You don't get it, do you? They're the animals. There's no reasoning with them.'

'At least let us try.' Jason was getting anxious.

'We don't have time to talk.' Laan was adamant. 'If you're not going to help, then leave us to shore up our defences.' She looked at the preparations taking place around her. 'We might not make it through the night, but perhaps we can take a few of them with us when we go.'

'That can never be the answer,' hissed Anne.

'You haven't lived through this,' Laan bellowed, suddenly confrontational. 'You know nothing of the fear we feel. Every night brings terror. We're captive here, completely at the whim of the humans. We're playthings to them. They torment us.'

There was an awkward silence.

'Where can we find them?' Jason asked, at last.

Laan shook her head, tutting disapprovingly. 'Over that ridge.' She pointed to the nearest rocky outcrop on the range of distant mountains. 'They've made themselves a home of their own about four kilometres away. A few of us have made it there to spy on them.' She shivered. 'Fewer of us have made it back.'

'Thank you,' said Anne, softly.

'Do what you will,' snapped Laan. 'I have preparations to make.'

She turned away from Jason and Anne, calling at some other animals for assistance.

Jason squeezed Anne's arm and looked deep into her eyes. 'Come on,' he said with a smile. 'Let's go save Paradise.'

A few of the creatures stood to watch as Intergalactic Rescue 4 lifted up into the evening sky. Most, however, were too engaged in their preparations to even notice.

Leaning on the controls, Jason swung the ship towards the mountain range.

'What are we going to do?' he asked.

'Appeal to their better natures,' Anne suggested. She tried her best to appear confident but her heart wasn't in it. 'If they *have* better natures.'

The two pilots passed the rest of the short journey in silence, the importance of their mission weighing heavily on their minds. The jungle outside the cockpit window got denser still as they headed towards the mountains. Looking down from their great height, Anne saw sparkling rivers and inviting pools through the canopy, as well as dramatic rocky outcrops and escarpments. Soon enough they were climbing to clear the mountain range they had seen in the distance. At the very top, Jason noticed a vast reservoir had been carved out of the rock. The mountains breached, he brought IGR4 skilfully through the clouds that had gathered at their highest peaks. As the ground came back into view beneath them, the small crew heard muffled thuds coming from the ship's hull.

'We appear to be under attack,' whistled Zeta.

'Anything to worry about?' Anne asked, concerned.

'Negative,' replied Zeta, much to Anne's relief. 'It appears to be a barrage of small projectiles.'

'Look there!' Jason was pointing out of the cockpit window. Turning, Anne saw a group of humans in a clearing. Some were running for cover as the ship approached, but others were manning wooden trebuchets. These sturdy machines were clearly capable of throwing rocks and stones a considerable distance.

'That's quite the welcome,' Jason sighed as he prepared to set down in the clearing.

'I suppose things can only get better from here,' said Anne, trying to look on the bright side.

Realising their resistance was futile, the humans had abandoned their trebuchet and retreated to the trees. As the exit ramp slid out from IGR4's hatch, Jason bravely took a step outside. He was rewarded with the thud of an arrow on the ship's hull, then another and another. He ducked back inside and bumped into Anne.

'I'm not sure this is such a good idea,' he breathed.

Before she could answer, Alpha limped past and onto the ramp. He stood for a few minutes at the halfway point as crude wooden arrows fell around him.

'He's drawing their fire,' said Anne in admiration of the little droid's courage. 'And they seem to be losing heart.'

Those few arrows that actually hit their mark bounced off Alpha's metal casing and fell harmlessly away. Sure enough, the barrage was slowing. In just a few minutes, it seemed their arrow supply was spent, or they had simply given up trying.

Jason took a breath and stepped outside again, his hands held high. 'We come in peace!' he called as, behind him, Anne rolled her eyes. She stepped out to join him.

'We're here to help!' she bellowed across the clearing. Peering into the trees, she could see dozens of shelters had been erected in their branches. Platforms and walkways hung from the lowest boughs while ladders made of twisted vines led up to the canopy.

'You are like us!' came a fearful voice from the trees.

Jason nodded. 'Yes!' he replied. 'We are human. From The League of Planets.'

There was a silence while the owner of the voice considered Jason's response. 'What are *planets*?' he called back, at last.

Jason looked at Anne, lost for words. 'They must have very short memories,' Anne shrugged.

Slowly, the tribe emerged from the trees. There were dozens of them of all ages; men, women and children. They were dressed in leaves and grasses but Anne could also see garments made of wool and cotton.

'What is the walking box?' asked an elderly man with a tattooed design on his neck.

Anne was confused. 'Walking box?' she muttered, looking around her. 'Oh! He means Alpha.' She raised her voice. 'It's a robot.' She could tell the man was none the wiser. 'A machine like your trebuchet,' she pointed to the weapon in the clearing, 'but with a brain like ours.'

'Surely they must remember robots?' Jason thought aloud. 'Laan said the colonists had only been here for 20 years. How can they not know about planets and robots?'

'Have you come to save us?' asked the old man.

'We have come to plead with you,' Jason clarified. 'To spare the lives of the defenceless animals.'

A few of the tribe laughed bitterly, and the elderly man held up his hand for silence. 'I think you had better sit down with us and talk.' He turned back to the trees, then had a final thought. 'But leave the walking box on your sky ship.'

For the second time in only a few hours, Jason and Anne found themselves sitting round a table laden with food. This time, they were several feet up on a platform in the trees. Anne noticed a difference in the air. Whereas a gentle breeze had blown in the animals' encampment, here the air was humid and still. She noticed many of the villagers around her were fanning themselves with great fronds to keep cool.

'I am Grell,' the old man said, 'the leader of our little tribe.'

'We have come to dissuade you from attacking tonight,' Anne explained, keen to cut to the chase. Looking up through the leaves, she could see the sky was darkening. It wouldn't be long before the full moon rose and the attack began.

'Attacking who?' the old man replied.

'The animals on the other side of the mountain,' Jason explained, suddenly confused. 'You have no right to drive them away.'

The man's eyes were wide. Once again, Anne noticed some of the tribespeople laughing to themselves. It was a wry laugh, as if they couldn't quite believe what Jason was saying.

'Look around you,' Grell said, suddenly throwing his arms wide. 'Do we look like we are ready to attack?'

Anne and Jason looked closer at the settlers and their village in the trees. Far from being ready for war, they seemed primed to defend themselves. For the first time, Anne noticed defensive rings of sharpened poles had been placed at the base of the trees. Jason saw that the trebuchet had been reloaded with boulders since they landed.

'But they told us—' Anne began, confused.

'They told you whatever they had to,' the old man interjected. 'No doubt your sky ship has formidable weapons?'

Jason nodded. 'They'd put your trebuchet to shame.'

Grell's eyes narrowed. 'And did they urge you to use them against us?'

'Yes, but only because they are desperate and afraid.' Anne looked around her, searching for an explanation for their strange predicament.

'They are desperate to be rid of us and have the planet for themselves.' There were murmurs of agreement at the old man's words. 'And if they are afraid of us, why do they attack us every night?'

Anne and Jason were dumbstruck. '*They* attack *you*?'

'Nightly,' the old man nodded. 'And they have done so ever since they arrived.'

Anne clutched at Jason's arm as her head began to swim. 'Since who arrived?' she gasped.

'The colonists, of course.' Grell gestured beyond the mountains with a bony finger. 'The animals, as you call them. Though they are more ferocious than any animal I ever met.'

Jason shook his head to clear it. 'Colonists?'

Grell sighed and sat back on the wooden platform. 'We are the indigenous species here. The dominant species, you might say.' He looked sad. 'Or, at least, we were. We have lived in peace for millennia here on Trilon. We work with Nature to provide everything we need. We respect the lesser species.'

'They said you wore their fur and ate their meat,' said Anne, suddenly angry.

'That is not so,' Grell assured her. 'As you can see, our clothes are made from the plants around us. We farm cotton and take the wool from our local fahl beasts – but only their wool. We are vegetarians, surviving on what we can forage from the jungle. Luckily, Nature provides us with much. And we repay the debt by respecting all her children. The animals, the plants, even each other.' Grell bowed his head. 'That is our philosophy, inherited from the generations that came before us.'

Anne was slowly piecing everything together. 'Then, when did the colonists come?'

'Some 20 years ago,' Grell explained, patiently. 'At first, they were our friends. At least, they pretended to be. They told us they came from a planet where the animals were dominant. They had technology beyond our comprehension.' He looked Jason in the eye. 'They came in a sky ship like your own.'

Jason nodded, suddenly understanding why their welcome had been less than cordial.

'Then,' Grell continued, 'their true intent became known.

It was to drive us from the planet and claim it as their own. I imagine they have done it many times before using similar methods. They seem well practiced.'

Anne was aghast. 'But they claim exactly the same of you!'

Grell spread his hands wide. 'Such are their methods.'

Anne noticed the nodding of many heads. 'The animals showed us proof of your attacks,' she said. 'Destroyed buildings and injured villagers.'

'They even showed us your demand that they should leave tonight. We saw it written on a wall.'

Grell smiled, slowly. 'But, none of us can write. We are a primitive people, we have no need for the written word.'

Anne and Jason shared a look. 'Then they deceived us,' Anne sighed.

'Utterly,' replied a Grell, a look of sorrow on his lined face.

'They wanted us to use our weapons against you,' Jason admitted.

'I am sure they did,' Grell nodded, sadly. 'We have been stubborn. We have proven more difficult to remove than they imagined. No doubt they thought your sky ship could do the job far more effectively.'

'We were determined to talk with you.' Anne insisted.

'Their leader tried to dissuade us,' Jason said.

'That does not surprise me in the least,' Grell admitted. 'Laan is the most duplicitous of them all.'

'So it was never their intention to be evacuated,' mused Anne, thinking through their initial meeting with Laan, 'no matter how big our ship.'

Jason picked up on her train of thought. 'Laan knew her distress signal would bring a ship from The League of Planets, and it was likely to bring some firepower with it.'

'You've got to help us.' Grell sounded suddenly desperate. 'If you leave, they will find a way to destroy us.'

Anne stood and walked to the edge of the platform, deep in thought. 'We could evacuate you.'

'Never!' came a shout from the assembled villagers. Others in the crowd took up the shout.

'Why should we leave our planet?' Grell thundered. 'If we leave, the colonists have won.' He took a breath to steel himself. 'This is our planet, our life. We will defend it to the death.'

'Then what do you suggest?' Jason asked, fearful of the answer.

'We know your sky ship has weapons,' Grell said, pointedly. 'Use them.'

'No!'

'But they don't belong here.' A woman with a young baby in her arms had stepped forward. "They threaten our very way of life.' She looked down at her infant. 'Our future.'

'They have no right!' came another voice.

'I think you must ask yourself,' began Grell, turning to Jason and Anne, 'whose side are you on?'

'We are on the side of peace,' Anne replied. 'Always peace.'

Grell shook his head, despondent. 'And how does that help us?'

'There is always another way,' Anne muttered, trying hard to convince herself.

'The reservoir,' said Jason suddenly. 'We flew over a reservoir on our way here.'

Grell nodded. 'We built it ourselves. Hewed the rock with our own hands. It took a generation, but the colonists soon diverted it to suit their own needs. Even in drought, they allow us nothing.'

Jason was thinking. 'Must hold a lot of water.'

Grell looked confused. 'Reservoirs generally do.'

The young pilot moved to Anne. 'I think I know a way to convince the animals to leave.'

'Jason,' Anne smiled, slyly. 'What do you have in mind?'

'A way to give them fair warning,' Jason grinned. 'And then to get them off this planet.'

'How will you do this?' The old man struggled to his feet. There was a flurry of excitement amongst the villagers.

'With the help of our walking box,' Jason winked.

As Intergalactic Rescue 4 took to the sky, Anne looked down on the little tribe. She was moved to see hope in their faces.

Jason interrupted her thoughts as he leaned on the controls. 'Zeet? Alpha? I want you to take as much explosive as you can from the armoury, then stand by in the cargo bay.'

The two robots scuttled from the flight deck.

'Anne, I'd like you to be ready with a volley of distress flares.'

Anne's heart was suddenly in her mouth. 'What's wrong?' she breathed.

'Nothing!' Jason laughed. 'But I want to attract the animals' attention before I flood their settlement.'

Anne's eyes grew wide. 'Before you *what?*'

'I'm going to flood their village.'

'But they'll be drowned,' Anne spluttered.

Jason shook his head. 'I don't think so.'

'Then where will they go?'

Jason set IGR4's nose to the horizon and the range of mountains ahead. 'If I'm right,' he smiled, 'they'll go home.'

He guided the ship to the top of the mountain. Just as IGR4 breasted the ridge, Anne gasped in awe. The sky was a dark blue. It looked like a sheet of velvet studded with sequins.

'The clouds have cleared.'

'Even better,' Jason grinned. 'They'll have a perfect view. Zeet? Alpha? You two ready?'

The two robots bleeped over the comms in acknowledgement.

'Great,' Jason replied, a note of excitement in his voice. 'Engage your thrusters as soon as the bay doors open. Standing by, Anne?'

Anne held her fingers poised over the emergency rescue console. 'Ready when you are.'

The bay doors opened and Zeta and Alpha began their descent. As they hit the reservoir wall, they cut power to their built-in thrusters and came to a rest on the rock. The two robots scanned the wall and found the areas of most weakness; small patches where cracks had begun to form.

'Got it,' Zeta reported over comms. 'If we plant an explosive pack on each of these fissures, they will produce enough energy to rupture the sides.'

'Approximately 41 mega joules, in fact,' Alpha interjected.

'More than enough!' came Jason's voice over their external speakers. 'Get to work!'

The two robots scuttled to the wall. Small hatch doors opened in their fronts and they each reached inside to produce packs of tightly wrapped explosives. They were placed carefully where they would do the most damage and the droids' hatches snapped shut.

'Ready,' bleeped Alpha, and the two droids engaged their thrusters.

'Okay, Anne,' came Jason's voice as they arrived safely in the cargo bay. 'Let's try and get their attention.'

Laan was addressing a crowd of animals around the fire.

'Our plans did not work,' she snarled, her yellow eyes burning bright. 'They did not buy our deception.' There were growls of derision from the assembled animals. 'But all is not lost!' The throng grew silent. 'We shall await their return, then storm their ship. They have powerful weapons. We will turn them on the humans and Trilon shall be ours! We will claim it for the Animal Empire!'

A great roar rose into the air. Animals of every shape and size threw back their heads and howled into the night sky. And that's when they saw the flares.

Great balls of coloured light traced their way through the sky, drawing the animals' eyes to the top of the mountain.

'What is that?' growled Laan.

'The rescue ship,' snarled a young beast. 'They're at the mountain.'

'What are they doing there?'

Her answer came in the form of four sharp cracks that echoed from the mountains. Even in the half-light, they could clearly see the debris thrown up by the explosions. Great cataracts of water spurted into the air before crashing back down onto the ridge.

'It's the reservoir!' brayed a wolf creature, saliva dripping from its jowls. 'They're going to flood our settlement!'

Already, they could hear the rumbling of water as it rushed down the mountainside. Laan knew they had only a few minutes before it crashed into their settlement. Everything would be swept away. It was doubtful any of them would survive.

'To the ship!' she called at the top of her lungs. 'It's our only chance!'

'We can't abandon Trilon to the humans,' growled a bear. 'We cannot let them win. We must make a stand for the Animal Empire!'

'You make a stand,' Laan snapped back. 'I'm getting out of here.'

She turned to join the hordes of other animals already running for the clearing. A large hatch slid aside leading to a ramp that plunged down into the sand. 'Start the engines!' she roared as she ran beneath the ground. 'Get us out of here!'

The bear turned back to the mountain to see a huge torrent of water smashing into the tree line. It was destroying everything in its path. Having second thoughts, the bear joined the last of the animal stragglers making their way down the ramp, seemingly into the bowels of the planet. The hatch slid shut. Suddenly, the ground began to shake. An ominous rumble filled the air, fighting with the roar of the approaching water for dominance. A great fissure appeared in the earth and, beneath it, came a glint of metal. As the earth and sand fell away, a huge ship was revealed, its rear engines glowing white hot. It heaved itself out of the clearing, clumps of vegetation falling from its hull. The strange craft turned a full 360 degrees, then spun away above the trees. A sudden blast from its aft engines and it was gone, the only evidence of its existence being a contrail of condensed air left hanging in its wake.

The moment it was gone, the water hit. A huge, unforgiving wave smashed into the settlement, lifting the buildings from their foundations. Great trees that had been uprooted and carried down the mountainside were thrown against the perimeter fence, breaching it as if it were made of string. Soon, there was nothing left of the village except a single wall of a single building, the writing on its side clearly visible in the starlight. BE GONE BY THE FULL MOON.

'How did you know?' Anne looked impressed as she watched the animals' ship blast into outer space.

Jason grinned. 'There was one question we never asked,' he replied. 'Where was the colonist's ship? They'd only been there 20 years, so they must have hidden it somewhere.'

'Did you know it was underground?' Anne swivelled her pilot's chair to face him.

Jason grinned as he remembered the feeling of the ground at the animals' village. 'Let's just say I had a hunch,' he beamed.

THE RECLUSE

A private message flashed up on Anne's monitor screen. Turning away, she glanced over her shoulder at her co-pilot. Jason was focused on steering the Pulse Drive through the interstitial space between stars. Any moment now the universe would tear apart, allowing them to cross the vast distance to their latest distress call.

'Trajectory confirmed,' read the message. 'Destination: ultimate location of covert communications.'

Her heart racing, Anne turned to where Alpha was blinking innocently in an alcove. She nodded slowly, then turned back to the screen to delete the little robot's message.

Over the previous weeks, Alpha had been tracing a set of secret communications sweeps from Intergalactic Rescue 4. He had determined that all their recent rescues had taken place within a narrow band of space – the direction of the signals. Anne gazed through the cockpit window as the stars resolved around them. Below them was a planet, spinning in the darkness, the source of the latest distress signal and, if Alpha was right, the ultimate destination of her co-pilot's transmissions. It seemed Jason was looking for something. And if that was the case, he might now have found it. Anne took a breath and looked at Jason by the controls. His face was unreadable. He had certainly been quieter than usual, but he was giving nothing away.

'The distress call is from a small 'hopper' class craft,'

reported Zeta as he plugged himself into IGR4's systems. 'It has come down in the Southern Hemisphere. Coordinates are incoming.'

'The planet is otherwise uninhabited,' Alpha interjected. 'Due to the extremes in climate, colonisation has never been attempted.'

Anne's eyes flicked to her co-pilot in readiness for a witty response. Nothing. Jason sat nodding in his chair, digesting the information. He gnawed his lip as he thought.

'Okay,' said Anne. 'Let's get down there.'

'We go carefully,' Jason said suddenly. 'I'll drive.' Tensing his jaw, he leaned into the controls and brought the ship about. Just as they entered the cloud layer, a torrent of rain smashed against the windscreen. Lightning flashed around them, illuminating the rolling clouds with an unearthly light. Suddenly, a crackle of static came over the ship's comms.

'Mayday,' came a woman's voice. 'Mayday. Can anybody read me?'

Anne flicked a switch on her comms panel. 'We read you,' she announced. 'This is Intergalactic Rescue 4 from The League of Planets. We have received your distress signal and are minutes away from making planetfall.'

'Oh, thank God,' came the voice again. 'But be careful. He's set a force field. It's what caused our crash. It affected our navigation control and then our engines.'

Anne blinked. 'Wait, what?' she spluttered. 'Who are you talking about? What force field?' She checked her screen for any sign of disturbance. Climatic data scrolled across the screen, but there was no sign of the energy build up she might expect to see from a force field.

Just as the woman responded, the signal was overcome with another burst of static. Anne could just pick out the odd word. 'Only hope... recluse... help me.' And then the comms went dead.

'Atmospheric interference,' Zeta explained.

'What was that all about?' Anne asked. Jason was silent, his gaze fixed through the cockpit window.

'I'm picking up two life signs in the crashed hopper,' Zeta reported. 'Neither is injured, but—— ' Zeta clicked and whirred as he paused mid-sentence.

'But what?' Anne was eager to hear.

'It appears one of them is very ill. I am picking up portable medical equipment on the hopper that seems to be keeping them alive.'

Anne frowned. 'Zeta, I want you standing by in the medbay. Alpha, you can come with me and Jason in case we need to cut them out.'

'The two of you should be enough,' Jason said suddenly. 'I'm going to investigate the source of that force field she spoke about.'

Anne was immediately suspicious. 'But I'm not picking anything up.'

'There are residual energy traces coming from over that ridge.' He nodded towards an escarpment that was rearing up before them. Anne could just make it out through the tempest.

She leaned forward to check her screen again. 'Could just be all this lightning,' she suggested as another flash lit up the sky outside.

'Maybe,' Jason conceded, 'but I still wanna check it out.' And, with that, he was silent once more.

Intergalactic Rescue 4 put down just a few metres away from the crash site. The rain showed no sign of letting up as Jason and Anne skulked down the ramp, Alpha scuttling along behind them. Almost immediately, Jason turned away from the mangled craft.

'Hey,' called Anne through the deluge. 'Aren't you going to stay and help?'

'I'll be right back,' Jason shouted back over his shoulder. 'I'm sure you and Alpha can manage.'

Anne glared at his retreating back, then turned to look at the damaged hopper. 'Okay, Alpha. Let's find a way in.'

The spaceship was about a quarter of the size of IGR4, just big enough to accommodate a small crew for a short journey. A leisure craft, really, mused Anne as she walked round to find an entrance, like those old-fashioned motorhomes she had seen in her history lessons.

'Here we go!' she called to Alpha. Wiping the rain from her eyes, Anne pointed to a door set into the side of the craft. The metal around it had buckled but the door remained intact and, by the looks of it, locked. Alpha extended a metal arm and connected himself to the control pad on the hull. He bleeped and whistled as he hacked into the ship's security systems. He didn't seem to mind the rain at all, thought Anne. She envied him.

At last, there came a whirring of machinery and the door slid aside with a hiss. Alpha retracted his arm and switched his visual sensors to torch mode. Limping ahead of Anne, he lit up the ship's interior in search of its occupants.

Anne heard a groan and turned to see a woman trapped beneath a twisted bulkhead. It was clear she had been thrown from the cockpit on impact.

'My leg,' she murmured, 'I can't feel my leg.'

Anne hurried to her and knelt at her side. 'It's okay,' she soothed. 'We're here.' She stroked stray strands of hair from the woman's bloodied face. There was a cut on her forehead. 'My name is Anne Warran.'

'I'm Treena Mai,' the woman gasped. 'Please, my daughter.'

'Your daughter?' Anne looked around, suddenly remembering Zeta saying he had detected two occupants in the craft.

'Nabi,' Treena nodded. 'She's in the medbooth. Please tell me she's okay.'

Alpha shone his torch around the cramped interior. At last, it rested on a raised coffin-like structure with cables and wires attached at various points. Anne stood up to investigate further. She ran her hand along the booth. It was made of a hardened plastic with a transparent lid. Anne cleared some debris aside to peer inside. Her heart skipped a beat. There, lying quite still with her eyes closed, was a young girl. She was dressed in a clinical, white gown. On her head, Anne saw a cap festooned with sensors. Looking up, she saw a monitor screen displaying live readings.

'Is she okay?' Treena asked.

'I think so,' Anne replied. 'Her stats seem fine.' She ran a finger over the transparent lid. 'There's a crack in the glass, but I think the unit's still sealed.'

'Thank God,' Treena laughed with relief. 'Please, can you free my leg so I can look at my girl?'

Alpha scuttled over the twisted bulkhead that lay across her lower body and shone his torch light on her legs.

'How does it look, Alpha?'

Alpha scanned the scene. 'I am detecting no breakages or lacerations,' he bleeped.

'Bruising only.'

'Then why can't I feel my legs?' groaned Treena.

'I'm sure it's just a trapped nerve.' Anne stroked her cheek to calm her. 'Can you clear it, Alpha?'

The little droid lit his oxy torch attachment and held it high. 'Affirmative,' he clicked. 'But I would recommend you look away.'

Anne squeezed Treena's hand as Alpha cut through the bulkhead. A shower of sparks lit up the craft's interior and the twisted metal glowed white hot. At last it fell in two, the larger piece breaking away to fall on the floor with a clang. Anne reached out to clear the smaller piece, then turned to Treena. 'You okay to stand now?'

'Yes,' exclaimed Treena with relief. 'The feeling's coming back.'

Anne reached out to help her to her feet. 'Here,' she said, 'put your weight on me.'

'Help me to my daughter,' Treena pleaded, and she hobbled to the medbooth with Anne's help. She lay her hand on the glass. 'I'm here, baby,' she said, softly. 'Mummy's here.'

'What's wrong with her?' Anne asked, gently.

Treena gazed into her daughter's face as she spoke. 'She has Luther's Syndrome. It's a condition that affects the brain. There's only one cure and it's outlawed in 30 systems.'

'Luther's Syndrome?' Anne murmured. She had never heard of it.

'No one knows what causes it,' Treena explained, a tear springing to her eye. 'It starts in the Limbic Lobe, the seat of the personality. Then it moves into the motor and nervous systems. Speech is taken away, then movement. I lost my little girl bit by bit.' Treena wiped her eyes with the back of her hand. 'She was terrified. Eventually, it leaves its victims as you see her now. Completely immobile, in a comatose state.'

Anne took her by the arm. 'But you said there was a cure?'

'Yes,' Treena nodded. 'And it's here. Here on this planet!'

'What is it? A plant? A chemical? You said it was outlawed.'

'Zetron radiation,' Treena replied.

Anne thought hard. Zetron radiation was deadly in the smallest quantity to everything but human life. It had been used as fuel for some experimental craft but had ultimately proven too dangerous. The Zetron powered ships had contaminated every planet they had visited. As a result, further research was halted and outlawed,

'There's Zetron radiation here?' Anne was confused.

Treena nodded. 'A targeted dose is the only thing that will cure my daughter. I detected trace amounts on this planet. Small, but enough to save her.'

'Then it's naturally occurring?' Anne wondered aloud.

'No.' Treena shook her head. '*He* has it.'

'Who?'

'The same man who set the force field. The same man who caused me to crash my hopper.'

'Er, Ms Warran,' beeped Alpha behind her, 'I have some more information on Zetron radiation. Information that might shed more light on Jason's covert transmissions.'

Intrigued, Anne squatted on her haunches to hear more. 'What is it, Alpha?' She wasn't sure she wanted to hear the answer.

'Intergalactic Rescue 1 was powered by Zetron radiation.'

Anne could feel her mind reeling. Jason had been sweeping space for IGR1's transponder signal. It seemed it had used a now outlawed form of energy for propulsion. Now Treena was telling her she had picked up a trace of Zetron radiation on this planet.

'Is it here?' Anne mused to herself. 'Has Jason found Intergalactic Rescue 1? And, if so, why?'

'I made contact from orbit with a man on the surface,'

Treena was saying. 'I explained that I needed access to Zetron radiation to save my daughter, but he refused permission for me to land.'

'He threw up the force field,' Anne nodded, 'and caused your hopper to crash.'

'Will you help me?' Treena was gazing at her.

'Of course,' Anne nodded. 'I'll radio my other droid, Zeta, to come and tend to Nabi. We need to get to the source of the radiation.' She looked at Treena with sudden pity. 'You're gonna get very wet.'

The rain, if anything, had got worse. It spattered on the ground around the little party as they walked and stung their eyes. With Alpha taking the lead, they made their way to the ridge. The little robot was sweeping the path ahead with a radiation detector. He had determined that the source of the force field was the same as the source for the Zetron radiation.

Squinting into the rain, Anne could see a crumpled shape on the ground just along the ridgeline ahead of them. As they got nearer, the shape resolved itself into the body of a young man.

'Jason!' Anne left the group to run ahead. As she squatted next to him, she saw him stirring.

'I've had enough of this rain!' he grunted, turning onto his side.

'What happened?' Anne reached out to wipe the water from his face.

'I guess I ran into the force field.'

'The same one that brought my hopper down.' Treena had joined them. She helped Anne lift Jason to his feet.

'You okay?' Anne asked, concerned.

Jason rubbed his eyes. 'I feel like I've gone eight rounds with a heavyweight boxer.' He shook his head. 'I'll be fine.'

'The source of the radiation and the force field is dead ahead,' bleeped Alpha. 'Approximately 40 metres.'

Anne blinked the rain from her eyes and lifted her gaze to beyond the ridge. A large, squat structure lay dead ahead. Anne gasped. Many modifications had clearly been made over the years. Extensions had been added to the original structure and towering antenna arrays had been mounted in the ground around it, but its original shape was still observable. Anne turned to Jason, a look of disbelief in her eyes.

'Intergalactic Rescue 1?'

Jason nodded, hardly daring to meet her gaze.

'You knew it was here.' Anne was aghast.

'I found it,' Jason acknowledged. 'I've been looking for a while.'

Anne decided to come clean in the belief it would prompt Jason to do the same. 'I know. Alpha's been tracking your transmissions.'

Alpha beeped sadly, as if he wasn't too happy at being drawn onto the argument.

'I thought I'd concealed them well enough,' Jason sighed.

'Oh, you're clever,' Anne smiled, ruefully, 'but not as clever as Alpha.' A happy whistle came from the little droid. 'What's in there?' Anne nodded to the stranded spaceship.

'Not what,' Jason replied. 'Who.'

'Master Stone, Ms Warran,' whirred Alpha, 'I have isolated the frequency of the force field.'

'Can you disable it?' Anne asked, hopefully.

'Affirmative,' bleeped Alpha. 'A sonic blast should disrupt it long enough for us to pass through.'

'Why are you so keen to get inside?' Jason asked, turning to his co-pilot.

Anne gestured to the woman behind them. 'This is Treena Mai,' she said. 'From the crashed hopper. Her daughter has a condition that can only be cured with Zetron radiation.'

Jason nodded in understanding and nodded towards the great hulk over the ridge. 'Well, you'll find plenty of it over there.'

Anne's eyes widened. 'So, it's true. IGR1 was powered by Zetron radiation.'

'It was The League of Planets' first experimental craft,' Jason explained, squinting into the rain, 'and the last to use Zetron radiation. It was found to be too dangerous. Deadly to anyone but humans. Any future use was banned under a Galactic treaty.'

Treena nodded. 'Which made my detection of it here on this planet all the more surprising.'

'But Intergalactic Rescue 1 went missing.' Anne was trying to remember everything she knew about the doomed mission. 'It was believed destroyed after slipping into a black hole.'

'Well, here it is,' said Jason. 'Doesn't look in too bad shape to me.'

'I am ready to instigate a sonic blast,' Alpha whistled. 'I would advise that you cover your ears.'

The little party did as they were instructed. A low rumble emanated from Alpha's casing. It gradually rose in pitch to become a piercing whistle. Even with her hands pressed against her ears, Anne felt like her bones were rattling. The force field became visible for a moment, sparking in the rain, then it failed.

'Force field disengaged,' Alpha reported happily as the

noise stopped. 'We have approximately 15 minutes until it remodulates.'

'Let's go,' breathed Jason, and he took a step over the ridge.

Thomas had watched the strangers approach on a monitor. From the appearance of their droid, he knew they had come from The League of Planets. He had supposed it was only a matter of time before they found him.

'Beta,' he barked. 'What's going on?'

A small, box-like droid trundled to his feet. A mechanical arm extended to a nearby console, connecting him to the ship and its monitoring systems. 'It looks like they have disabled the force field,' he bleeped. 'Funny,' he mused as he analysed the data. 'That's just what I would have done.'

Thomas put his head in his hands. 'Why don't they just leave me alone?' he sighed.

'No matter,' whistled Beta. 'We have other defences.'

'It's been here some time,' Anne mused as they approached the beached ship.

'It went missing 10 years ago,' said Jason. 'I was seven.'

Anne nodded. 'If memory serves, it had only one human crew member aboard and a single droid.'

Jason was striding ahead. 'After IGR1,' he called over his shoulder, 'The League of Planets reconfigured the Pulse Drive to use safer fuel. But nothing was ever heard from this ship again.'

Anne halted in her tracks. 'How do you know all this? There's no record of IGR1 in the official databases.'

Jason shrugged. 'I grew up with it.'

Just as he was about to take a step forward, Treena called from behind them. 'Stop!'

Anne turned to see her pointing to her feet. Following her gaze, she saw something sticking up from the ground. The driving rain had washed some of the topsoil away, revealing a small, metallic point.

'What is that?' Anne panted.

'I don't know,' replied Treena, her eyes scanning the ground ahead. 'But there's more of them.'

Looking around, Anne saw at least a hundred more of the tiny objects scattered at their feet. She guessed there must be many more that the rain hadn't yet revealed. 'Alpha?'

In response, the little robot opened a small vent in the top of his head. In the driving rain it wasn't long before he had filled an internal reservoir. He extended a nozzle to the ground and squirted water carefully around the object, clearing it of mud. It was a small metallic disc, just 20 centimetres in diameter.

'Proximity mine,' Alpha whistled.

'Whoever's in there, they're really not keen on having company, are they?' Anne shook her head in disbelief.

Jason picked up a large stone from the ground and threw it into the air above one of the mines. A laser beam hissed from the central nib, shattering the stone into a hundred pieces. Almost simultaneously, every other mine sent their lasers into the air, fizzing and popping in the torrential rain.

'I remember these,' said Jason. 'They're museum pieces now but we covered them in my military history module at the Academy.'

'Let me guess,' Anne scoffed. 'You came top?'

'Where else?' Jason beamed.

Anne put her hands on her hips, inviting him to try. 'I know you love a challenge.'

Jason turned to the little droid at his feet. 'Alpha? Toolkit, please.'

A hinged lid sprung open in Alpha's front revealing an array of small tools secured with clips. Kneeling in front of the robot, Jason selected a slender tool resembling a long needle with a kink at its point, then lay on his stomach to tinker with the mine. Anne couldn't help but smirk as the rain splashed mud into his face.

'The trick is to go in underneath,' Jason was saying as he dug carefully beneath the object, excavating the mud with his device. 'And to be sure it doesn't move.'

At last he had dug a small tunnel beneath the mine. Holding the tool in front of him, he turned the handle. The end of the needle began to glow. 'These mines can't detect heat,' he explained. 'They don't have to. So heat is the perfect weapon to use against them.' Biting his tongue as he worked, he carefully probed the bottom of the mine with the white-hot needle. 'They operate on a shared wireless network,' he whispered carefully. 'If one of them is activated, it alerts all the others.' With an almost imperceptible turn of his hand, he manipulated a toggle on the bottom of the mine. 'The heat can disrupt the network and reverse it.' The toggle gave a soft click. 'So, if one of them goes to sleep, they all go to sleep.' With a final movement, the little nib retracted back into the mine, leaving its surface smooth and shining. Wiping the rain from his face, Jason reached out carefully to the device and scooped it up in his hands as if it were a piece of fragile glass. Suddenly, he threw it into the air above a string of other mines. Nothing. It fell to the ground like a stone.

'There,' said Jason as he rose to his feet. 'Piece of cake.'

'You weren't sure that was going to work, were you?' Anne gasped.

'Perhaps not entirely,' Jason admitted.

'But I thought you said you'd come top of your class?'

Jason shrugged. 'Well, I'm sure I would have done if I'd turned up for the exam.' He winked as he returned his tool to Alpha and bent over to try and wipe the worst of the mud from his clothes. 'Onward?' he beamed.

The monitor flickered and popped. Thomas brought his fist down on top to stabilise the image. It rolled for a moment before settling into a steady view of the area outside the ship. He had watched as the little party defeated another of his defences.

'They're persistent,' he sighed, 'I'll credit them with that, at least.'

'They are showing extraordinary guile,' Beta agreed.

Thomas scratched at the stubble on his chin. Something was bothering him. 'Beta,' he rasped, 'could you rewind?'

At his command, the image stopped and rewound. 'Stop!' Thomas barked. He leaned in closer to the screen. 'Zoom in there.' He pointed to a corner of the screen where the male in the group was laying on the ground, tampering with the proximity mine. Beta zoomed in on the young man's face. The image lost definition as he did so and the torrential rain distorted the image further but, still...

'It can't be,' Thomas whispered to himself. Many years had passed, of course, but he was sure he recognised that jaw and hairline. With a deep frown, he swivelled in his chair to a ramshackle table next to him. Reaching out, he snatched at an old photograph in a tarnished frame. It was a picture of a young boy, perhaps 7 years old, clutching a toy spaceship resembling Intergalactic Rescue 1.

'Jason.'

Anne was tired of the rain. It beat down on them with a remorselessness that was hard to bear. 'Do you think it's always like this?'

Jason turned to her, his hair plastered to his head and rivulets of water running into his eyes. 'Zeta did say the climate had kept settlers away.'

'I can't imagine why anyone would stay here.' She nodded towards the ship ahead of them. 'Why didn't they just leave?'

Jason pointed to the ruptured engine units to the rear of the ship. 'I don't think they had a lot of choice in the—— ' His words were cut short by a sudden rumbling sound. Anne was sure the ground was shaking beneath their feet. She swung her arms out to steady herself as the earth gave way ahead of them.

'What now?' Looking to her left and right, she saw a great trench was opening up, encircling the spaceship. As the ground settled, the little party was now faced with a defensive moat, some four feet wide. Much too wide to jump. Peering over the side, Anne saw the sides and floor of the trench were covered in horrible, jagged spikes.

'Great,' she sighed. 'Perhaps we should just turn back. Fire up IGR4 and find a way in from the air.'

'No!' protested Treena. 'We are not giving up. My daughter's life depends on us getting inside that ship.'

'You're right.' Anne nodded, suddenly sheepish. She walked a few steps to peer round the front of the craft. 'It's the same all the way around.' This close, she could just make out movement through the ship's cockpit window. 'Well,' she muttered, 'whoever's in there, they know we're here. I bet they're really enjoying this.'

'Does your droid have a laser?' Treena asked, thinking fast.

Alpha whistled, sadly.

'Not that powerful,' Jason answered for him.

'A winch line?'

Alpha beeped happily. 'All units have a projectile winch cannon fitted as standard,' he whistled.

Treena pointed to an antenna array that stood beyond the trench. 'Could you reach that and pull it down? It must be all of six metres high.'

Almost before she had finished speaking, a tiny flap had opened in Alpha's chest unit. With a puff of explosives, a line unspooled at speed through the rain. With a clang, the hook at the end wrapped itself around the antenna and held fast. With the line taut, a drill bit suddenly appeared on Alpha's underside. It bore its way through the ground, holding the little robot steady against the tension of the wire. Now secure, Alpha began to wind the line in. Slowly, the antenna began to bend at its base. The robot's internal motor protested as it strained against the solid metal, and Anne was sure she could see steam rising from his internal mechanisms. Finally, the antenna snapped and the tall mast fell to the ground. It straddled the trench with ease.

'Good work!' Jason enthused as he led the little party across. The antenna was sturdy enough, but Anne still got a shiver as she crossed. The thought of those spikes beneath her was almost too much to bear. Once on the other side, Jason extended a hand to help Anne and Treena across. Alpha, he noticed, had engaged his own built-in thrusters and was crossing the trench in his usual inimitable fashion.

'I'm glad to see you still have your manners.'

The voice cut Jason to the core. Turning where he stood, he saw a ramp had extended from the ship's entrance. There, in the hatch, stood a sturdy, middle-aged man with grey hair and stubble. He had changed considerably over the last few years, but the voice was still unmistakeable. 'Hello, Jason.' There was a catch in the man's throat as he spoke.

The effect on Jason was immediate. The colour draining from his face, he fell to his knees in the mud.

'Jason!' exclaimed Anne, suddenly worried for her friend. 'Who is that man?

Jason's voice was as weak as the man's was strong. 'That's my father,' he whispered.

Thomas Stone was the picture of sorrow. 'I have so much to apologise for,' he said. Although he was trying hard to fight it, his eyes were pricked with tears. 'For leaving you as a boy, and for treating you as a common intruder.' He lifted his eyes to meet Jason's gaze. 'But this place is dangerous.'

Jason nodded and reached out a hand. 'We know.'

'My coming here destroyed all life on this planet.' He turned to a computer console and called up a file. Data scrolled across a cracked monitor screen. 'I worked out the Pulse Drive was leaking Zetron energy,' he rasped, his voice thick with emotion. 'This whole planet was once teeming with primitive life. Now it's all gone.'

Anne smiled. 'Zetron energy is deadly to everything but human life.'

Thomas' eyes grew wide with horror. 'Then my suspicions were correct.' He lifted a hand to cover his face. It was almost too much to contemplate.

'But you couldn't have known that, Father,' Jason soothed. 'We only discovered that once IGR1 had disappeared.'

'It's not your fault,' Anne added.

'Have you been here for 10 years?' Jason was looking unbearably sad.

Thomas nodded. 'It feels like much longer. I crashed

here when we fell through the black hole. It was a conduit to another part of the galaxy. The ship's engines were damaged beyond repair.' He leaned up against the console. 'At first I farmed the land, determined to live in harmony with the environment. Luckily, I stored enough grain and pulses to last me if I ate sparingly. The ship's bays are full of dried food.' He took a breath. 'Then everything outside died. I knew I could never get home, but that nothing could ever be allowed to come to this planet. I had done enough damage.' He reached out a trembling hand to stroke Jason's cheek. 'I have missed so much.'

Jason's lip trembled. 'There's still time.'

There was a silence as they both contemplated the lost years. 'How is your mother?' Thomas asked at last.

'She's well,' Jason smiled. 'And she'll be very pleased to see you.'

'Does The League know you've found me?'

'Not yet,' Jason sniffed. 'They deleted all records of IGR1 from their databases.'

Thomas let his hand fall. 'I'm an embarrassment.'

'You're a hero,' Anne corrected him. 'And you'll return home as such. The League of Planets must own their mistakes as well as their triumphs.'

'You mustn't blame yourself,' Treena smiled. 'What you consider deadly may yet save a life.'

Thomas raised his eyes.

Treena continued. 'My daughter is suffering from a condition that can only be cured by Zetron radiation.' She stood, a sudden sense of urgency in her voice. 'She is in a medbooth on my hopper. I detected traces on this planet but your force field brought my ship down.'

Thomas shook his head. 'Forgive me,' he pleaded. 'I was

trying to keep you away. I've been trying to keep everyone away."

'Is that how you have lived all these years?' Anne asked, sadly. 'Totally alone?'

Thomas cast his eyes over to where Alpha and Beta were busy synching their systems. 'Not totally,' he said with a smile.

'Alpha, Beta,' said Jason suddenly, 'could you reconfigure the Pulse Drive to deliver a targeted dose of Zetron radiation?'

Alpha bleeped. 'Sure, if we have the right equipment.'

'We could use the antenna you pulled down as an emitter,' whistled Beta.

Alpha hummed, happily. 'That's just what I was going to say.'

It took a supreme effort on everyone's part to build the emitter. As Alpha and Beta completed the task, the humans busied themselves filling in a portion of the trench, all in the driving rain.

'Does this ever stop?' yelled Anne above the noise of the storm.

'Sure!' Thomas called back. 'For two days every three years.'

Anne groaned and bent to her task. A section of the Pulse Drive was removed and attached to the makeshift emitter. At the flick of a switch, it hummed with a latent energy. 'Zetron radiation,' Thomas announced. 'Targeted and fired from the very end of this modified antenna.' He turned to the two robots. 'I gotta tell ya, you two guys make a great team!'

The journey back to Treena's hopper was arduous with the emitter in tow, but they all knew there was a lot riding on its safe delivery. As Jason and his father manhandled the equipment up the ramp and through the hatch, and Treena busied herself at the controls of her daughter's medbooth, Alpha introduced Zeta to his new friend. He was so excited, he even forgot to pretend he had a limp.

'Okay,' panted Jason. 'It's secure.'

Anne helped Treena attach the ramshackle machine to the medbooth, the emitter placed just a few centimetres from Nabi's skull. At the flick of its switch, the emitter hummed back to life. With reference to the monitor screen, Treena was able to position it precisely so that the radiation would be delivered to exactly the right spot in Nabi's brain.

'Here goes,' she whispered, suddenly nervous. She leaned over to lay a hand on her daughter's forehead. 'Please get better, baby.'

Moving her hand to the console, she directed the machine to fire pulse after pulse of Zetron radiation into Nabi's skull. As the process continued, Treena was able to monitor the situation on her screen. 'It's working!' she exclaimed. 'The damage is repairing!'

The little party clapped their hands in triumph. The operation complete, Treena moved the equipment out the way and leaned into the medbooth. Carefully removing Nabi's skull cap with all the sensors attached, she laid her hand on her daughter's chest.

'Honey?' she whispered. 'Nabi? Can you hear me?'

After what seemed an age, Nabi slowly opened her eyes. Treena caught her breath as she saw something she had been certain she would never see again. Her daughter's smile.

'He limps because he thinks it makes him seem important.' Zeta was chatting merrily to his new-found friend as Alpha busied himself with a maintenance task. 'Because he is older, he thinks he is the superior robot.'

'Well,' bleeped Beta, 'I'm the second oldest. Perhaps I should have a limp too.'

Zeta buzzed in warning. 'Let's not ruin his day, huh?'

They whistled together as they trundled to the flight deck. Once there, Zeta let out a mechanical arm and plugged himself into the ship's controls. 'Where to, Master Stone?' he asked.

Jason and Anne looked at each other as they snapped on their restraints, then turned in their chairs to face Thomas.

'What do you think, Dad?' Jason asked. 'Wanna see a bit of the galaxy?'

Thomas smiled. 'I think I've seen enough for now.' He looked suddenly thoughtful. 'I think it's time I faced the music. Let's go home.'

Jason nodded in agreement. 'Let's do that,' he said and turned back to the navigation controls. 'Okay, Zeet, you heard the man. Punch in the coordinates for Earth and let's get outta here!'

As the little robot clicked and whirred, a hole in the very fabric of space opened up before them. With a blast of energy from the Pulse Drive, Intergalactic Rescue 4 seemed to teeter on the edge for a while. Then, as the stars blurred around it, it slipped effortlessly through.

AUTHOR'S NOTE

When I was first presented with Intergalactic Rescue 4 for adaptation, I knew that some changes would be required. Originally conceived as a ten-part television series for children, I needed it to spring from the page as a collection of short stories.

My first decision was to include a loose arc that would bind the stories together and reach its denouement in the final tale (the 'series finale', as it were). None of the stories needed changing to fit the arc particularly, so it was a simple matter of seeding it throughout the series.

Where they did need changing, it was to solve problems of narrative (how did such and such a spaceship get to such and such a planet), problems of science (how would going faster than light cause people to 'de-age') or problems with missing pages in the original treatment (see 'Space Train', below).

Other considerations included addressing the gender balance. I make no apologies for turning male characters female, not in an attempt to be 'PC' or (heaven forbid) 'woke', but to simply reflect the world we live in – and, more likely, the one that Anne and Jason would live in many years from now.

In any event, I thought it would be interesting for the reader to see just what I changed and why. Here, then, is a brief summary of the stories that you have just read detailing how Gerry Anderson and Fred Freiberger would have liked you to see them and how, in my audacity, I have changed them. It is for you to decide if I was right.

The Slave Trader

I changed very little in this first story (although, in the original running order, it was the third story) except the logistics of the rescue. Specifically, dumping the fuel before cutting the fuel line. This was conceived as a nice story about conscience and what happens when bad people decide, in the end, to do a good thing. I hope it remains just that.

Space Train

This was presented to me with the last page missing. Despite Jamie's best efforts, it just could not be found. So, it was left to me to provide an ending. I thought the idea of the Vulcans deliberately sabotaging the train was a neat one. And top marks to Gerry and Fred for having the audacity to use that particular alien race! I suppose it must be remembered that, at this stage, Star Trek was a distant television memory, its big screen rebirth still yet to come.

Second Chances

This is a recurring theme in the original stories, that of someone bad being persuaded to do something good. The aliens' 'de-aging' proved to be particularly problematic. In the original treatment it happened when IGR4 jumped to faster than light speed. *'In other words,'* Gerry and Fred say, *'they begin to get younger (Einstein's theory in reverse)'.* Now, I'm no expert on Einstein's Special Theory of Relativity but this simply didn't work for me. Far better, I thought, to have the very thing they were stealing being the cause of their problems. I thought the original ending was rather weak, too, with the evil alien (I have called him Nev) being 'subdued'. I felt he should pay for his villainy, and so I had him die trying to complete the theft having been offered his second chance.

The Saboteur

Originally called 'The Rogue Android Story', this is essentially intact as the original document intended, although it was my idea that the two races be defined by their different colours of hair and dress – and for Moran to combine the two to show how the one race had diverged. In fact, in the original story, he doesn't appear at all. No explanation is given for the strange android, it is simply a means to get the two races working together to prevent a disaster. I thought it would be a neat idea that he was a 'fail safe programme', implanted by the original engineer in case of emergency.

Double Exposure

I changed very little here although it was my invention that Godrick should hijack IGR4 towards the end of the story and that Zestor and Kelix (unnamed in the original) should be married. I mean, wouldn't you want to spend three years on a lunar outpost, light years from the nearest habitable planet, with your spouse? You don't have to answer that!

The Troglodytes

Primitive societies living underground or worshipping false gods are a familiar theme in the original treatment (see *The Slave Trader* and below, *Animals*), to the point that the idea becomes a little repetitive. I tried to put a bit more flesh on the bones of the Troglodytes themselves in terms of character, and also introduced the idea of one of them, Jaxim, having the courage to question the prevailing religious 'wisdom' in the name of science, an idea of which I'm sure Gerry would have approved. I felt the original idea of IGR4 going back in time to observe a primitive planet was redundant – once you introduce time travel into any story, you're heading into trouble. After all, the reader thinks, why can't they just go back in time whenever they want to put things right? Far simpler, I thought, for them just to be observing a primitive planet in their own time.

The Stowaway

The treatment for this story is a whacking seven pages long. This compares to most of the others which run to two, three or four pages. Because it was so fleshed out, I was able to relax and essentially add the dialogue and action as required. I particularly enjoyed bringing Kran's authoritarian regime to life, and the rescue on the bridge at the beginning – an event that happens before the story even starts in the original treatment. Like in most of the stories, this ends with a sweet exchange between Alpha and Zeta concerning the more confusing aspects of human nature. And, like in most stories, I decided to cut it.

Ice Moon

This sailed dangerously close to being too similar to *Double Exposure* (above), with the main threat to the base being the encroaching ice with the coming of the lunar night. It was my idea that Hoshi should risk her life to save Cramer's data and that her potential sacrifice might bring them closer together – and that they should both be female rather than male. No apologies for that.

Animals

This was fun. The original story had Jason and Anne meeting the humans first and them claiming to be the colonists on the planet. They report having trouble with the indigenous animals who refuse to accept their overlords. The animals are a primitive culture living in caves (see also *Second Chances* and *The Troglodytes*). Ultimately, a rescue involving their leader helps to bring the two races together. I thought it would be interesting to meet the animals first and to have *them* claim that they are the indigenous population. Our assumptions can then be turned on their heads when we meet the humans, the *real* indigenous species. It then became a matter of getting the animals off the planet (I thought the original idea of the subjugated species learning to live with their new masters rather unlikely), and so I invented the reservoir, the plan to flood the village (with a few Derek Meddings inspired explosions) and the escape in a buried spaceship.

The Recluse

This was quite a simple story in the original treatment and so became the perfect vehicle for me to wrap up the series arc – Jason's covert search for his father. Originally, the recluse was simply that; a grumpy man who had to be convinced to provide medicine to a dying child. With Thomas Stone as the recluse, there was now a more convincing reason why he would shun society; his belief that Intergalactic Rescue 1 was a danger to others. Once again, a man and his son from the original treatment became female characters, Treena and Nabi, with no discernible effect on the merits of the story.

OTHER GREAT TITLES
FROM ANDERSON ENTERTAINMENT

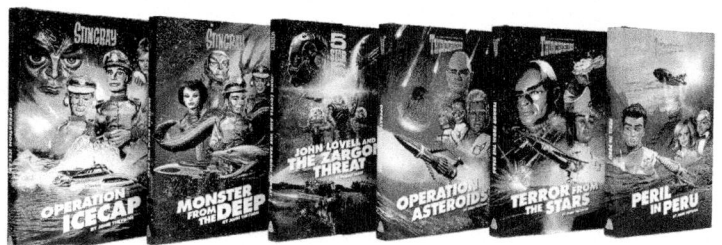

STINGRAY

Stingray: Operation Icecap

The Stingray crew discover an ancient diving bell that leads them on an expeditionary voyage through the freezing waters of Antarctica to the land of a lost civilisation. Close on the heels of Troy Tempest and the pride of the World Aquanaut Security Patrol is the evil undersea ruler Titan. Ahead of them are strange creatures who inhabit underground waterways and an otherworldly force with hidden powers strong enough to overwhelm even Stingray's defences.

Stingray: Monster from the Deep

Commander Shore's old enemy, Conrad Hagen, is out of prison and back on the loose with his beautiful but devious daughter, Helga. When they hijack a World Aquanaut Security Patrol vessel and kidnap Atlanta, it's up to Captain Troy Tempest and the crew of Stingray to save her. But first they will have to uncover the mystery of the treasure of Sanito Cathedral and escape the fury of the monster from the deep.

A GERRY ANDERSON PRODUCTION

Thunderbirds: Operation Asteroids

What starts out as a simple rescue mission to save a trapped miner on the moon, soon turns out to be one of International Rescue's greatest catastrophes. After the Hood takes members of International Rescue hostage during the rescue, a chase across space and an altercation among the asteroids only worsens the situation. With the Hood hijacking Thunderbird Three along with Brains, Lady Penelope and Tin-Tin, it is up to the Tracy brothers to stage a daring rescue in the mountain tops of his hidden lair. But can they rescue Brains before his engineering genius is used for the destructive forces of evil?

Thunderbirds: Terror from the Stars

Thunderbird Five is attacked by an unknown enemy with uncanny powers. An unidentified object is tracked landing in the Gobi desert, but what's the connection? Scott Tracy races to the scene in the incredible Thunderbird One, but he cannot begin to imagine the terrible danger he is about to encounter. Alone in the barren wilderness, he is possessed by a malevolent intelligence and assigned a fiendish mission – one which, if successful, will have the most terrifying consequences for the entire world. International Rescue are about to face their most astounding adventure yet!

Thunderbirds: Peril in Peru

An early warning of disaster brings International Rescue to Peru to assist in relief efforts following a series of earth tremors – and sends the Thunderbirds in search of an ancient Inca treasure trove hidden beneath a long-lost temple deep in the South American jungle!

When Lady Penelope is kidnapped by sinister treasure hunters, Scott Tracy and Parker are soon hot on their trail. Along the way they'll have to solve a centuries-old mystery, brave the inhospitable wilderness of the jungle and even tangle with a lost tribe – with the evil Hood close behind them all the way...

SPACE: 1999 Maybe There –
The Lost Stories from SPACE: 1999

Strap into your Moon Ship and prepare for a trip to an alternate universe!

Gathered here for the first time are the original stories written in the early days of production on the internationally acclaimed television series SPACE: 1999. Uncover the differences between Gerry .and Sylvia Anderson's original story Zero G, George Bellak's first draft of The Void Ahead and Christopher Penfold's uncredited shooting script Turning Point. Each of these tales shows the evolution of the pilot episode with scenes and characters that never made it to the screen. Wonder at a tale that was NEVER filmed where the Alpha People, desperate to migrate to a new home, instigate a conflict between two alien races. Also included are Christopher Penfold's original storylines for Guardian of Piri and Dragon's Domain, an adaption of Keith Miles's early draft for All That Glisters and read how Art Wallace (Dark Shadows) originally envisioned the episode that became Matter of Life and Death.

Discover how SPACE: 1999 might have been had they gone 'Maybe There?'

Five Star Five: John Lovell and the Zargon Threat

THE TIME: THE FUTURE
THE PLACE: THE UNIVERSE

The peaceful planet of Kestra is under threat. The evil Zargon forces are preparing to launch a devastating attack from an asteroid fortress. With the whole Kestran system in the Zargons' sights, Colonel Zana looks to one man to save them. Except one man isn't enough.

Gathering a crack team around him including a talking chimpanzee, a marauding robot and a mystic monk, John Lovell must infiltrate the enemy base and save Kestra from the Zargons!

available from
shop.gerryanderson.com

Printed in Great Britain
by Amazon

18301446R00133